He Calls Me Wifey: A Hood Love Story

By: Theresa Reese

Synopsis:

What do you do when the one you love may be the one you should hate? Love comes with ebbs and flows, but when it comes with possible betrayal, it's toxic and possibly deadly.

Meet Kori. She's more than eye candy and comes with baggage that Edo doesn't know he can handle.

Edo, the nephew of a top record label executive, He has his eyes set on taking over once his uncle steps down. Deuce, however, has options. One being Diesel, his nephew's best friend who doesn't know what's going on but wants to take charge.

As secrets unfold, trust withers away. Even if it's with the one you want to give your all to.

Will Kori and Edo beat the odds and discover a way to have it all or will personal family vendettas get in the way. Love can be more than enough when love is all you want, but when there is more on the line, a deadly

end may be the outcome.

Find out if Kori and Edo can survive this Hood love story.

Prologue

"You have a prepaid call from Edo at The Greene Correctional Facility, this call may be monitored or recorded for quality purposes."

Hearing the automated machine end the message, I was eager to hear from the love of my life.

"Wassup mami," Edo spoke into the phone, causing my heart to swell.

Smiling from ear to ear, I responded, "Hey papi."

"Sup witchu, you miss a nigga?"

"Edo, you know I miss you so stop talking foolish." Sitting on the white chaise that sat in the middle of my She-shed, I got comfortable as I listened to the man I'd grown to love over the past few months.

"Where that bitch at?" Edo asked.

Peeking up, I knew it was only a matter of minutes before he brought her up. Hearing the venom in his voice, I reassured him I was alone. "Papi relax, you have my undivided attention. I miss you tho and I want to see you so bad!" I tried soothing him.

"So, make it happen ma. Don't talk about it, be about it."

After 15 minutes, I heard the familiar keys jingle. I knew it was none other than Ari. "Baby, I have to go."

"You have 2 minutes left," the automated voice interrupted.

"Kori, you better not end this call before the machine say my time is up," he chastised.

Looking up, I figured I had better think fast if I didn't want her to hear me talking to Edo. Jumping up to close and lock the door, she appeared, pushing her way in. Dropping the phone in a panic, I heard Edo's voice booming through the speaker.

"Hey, baby girl."

Realizing my phone was still on a call, Ari picked up the phone, looking at the number that she had told me to block weeks ago. Turning on her heels, she placed the phone to her ear. "Didn't I say to stay away from my bitch, your days are numbered Edo. Try me if you want to, while I got you by your balls," she spat.

"Bitch, you got me fucked-," the call ended.

Looking up at Ari with pleading eyes, she rushed to my side, yoking me up. "You got me fucked up if you think I'ma let you talk to this nigga like ain't nothing wrong…"

Rewind...

Chapter 1

Kori

"Kori, are you mad at me?" Ari asked, trying to pull me into her embrace.

Fed up was an understatement. Time and time again, I had to battle with myself, wondering if I was making the right move by dating Ari. Looking over my shoulder at my girlfriend of the past 4 years, I couldn't do anything but roll my eyes at her dramatics. "Ari, just leave me alone right now. When I'm ready to deal with your ass, I will!"

Hopping up from the bed, I slipped my feet in my UGG plush slippers, grabbed my robe that laid across the chair and headed straight to the bathroom to freshen up. Ari had been coming home later and later every night with a sad excuse to why she had to stay at work late. I wasn't buying the bullshit she tried to feed me.

Tonight, I'd be celebrating my promotion at my job with my girls Kristen and Jada, so Ari could keep her drama-filled ass home tonight. Picking up my phone, I dialed Kristen's number.

"Hola mami."

"Hey chick, you ready for tonight?"

"Yea, and I'd be better if Ari would stop pressing me about what spot we going to. I really just want to be around y'all without her tagging along, getting on my nerves," I stressed.

"Tell her ass you don't know cuz you know I'm not telling that bitch nothing; she can stay her ass home for a damn change," Kristen said. "But, you better be ready at 10, Koriann. I'm not going to be waiting all night for you to figure out what you're going to wear."

Rolling my eyes at the ceiling, I answered, "I understand." I ended the call before my older sister, Kristen, could start questioning why I wasn't inviting my girlfriend to my celebration.

Ari had an issue with being controlling and insecure, but tonight was not the night to deal with that. I was the youngest real estate agent in my company, not to mention I was a minority. After busting my ass for 3 years at the age of 26, I was making over $100,000, had my own 3 bedroom condo in Yonkers, and pushing a 2019 Audi A6 so, in other words, I was a Boss Bitch. Ari, on the other hand, was 32, a police officer who seemed to always get mixed up into drama, which caused her to either have to take unpaid leaves or suspension. Talk about women age faster than men, well not when it came to this chick. If she wasn't a beast in the bedroom, I would have left her ass a long time ago.

"So, where exactly are you going Kori?" Ari asked as she stood on the opposite side of the bathroom door, probably eavesdropping on my convo.

"Ari, I don't fucking know. Damn, my girls are taking me out!" Throwing up my hands in defeat, I walked past her as she had her arms folded across her chest.

"Cut the bullshit Kori, you just don't want me to show up and stop them niggas from drooling over your thick ass."

Walking up on me, I already knew Ari wasn't going to let this shit go. "Fine, you wanna come, then be ready by 9 Ari, not a minute more. And if you fuck up my night, I swear this relationship," pointing in between the both of us, "is dead," I stressed, bumping past her.

Still not understanding why I decided to deal with Ari after all the arguments and fights, I just couldn't seem to completely cut her off. My best friend, Jada, couldn't stand the sight of Ari, so I knew I had to warn her of the invitation I had just extended to her. Jada knew about the fights and always told me I shouldn't tolerate it when I was better off without her, but I had a soft spot for Ari and something drastic had to change my mind.

Later that night...

"Bitch, don't you look like a bad bitch!" Jada sang from the driver's seat of her blue BMW 3 Series.

Strutting, I showed off my outfit of choice for the night. I decided on an Olive Venus and Mars jumpsuit from Milano, nude Giuseppe Zanotti strap sandals, and complemented with my mini Chanel flip bag. Flipping my shoulder length curls over my shoulder, I winked at my girls while popping my gum. Standing at 5'2" with wide hips, small waist, ample ass, and c cup perky breasts, my blonde hair was pinned with deep wave curls, showing off my bronze skin.

"Hurry your ass up," Kristen chastised, cutting my runway walk short.

"Why you always hating?" I shot back, opening the back door.

"Cuz you always showing out," Ari whispered in my ear.

Shooting her a menacing glare, I knew I should have left the bitch home. Making it to the club in less than 30 minutes, I wanted to head straight to the bar for a drink. Not one to drink anything more than wine, I was in dire need of a few shots of Hennessy.

"We got us a spot in VIP!" Kristen yelled out to me, but I continued stepping towards the bar."

Nodding at her to let her know I heard, I ordered two shots of Henny with Ari in tow. With her being a police officer, you would think that she would wanna keep a low profile but, no, she had to make her presence known.

Ari was taller than me, standing at 5'8" and 170 pounds of ass and hips, which was what immediately drew me to her. Her complexion was caramel coated and she possessed these dark brown almond shaped eyes that were hypnotizing to say the least. I wasn't into AG's, as they were called here in New York; I needed a bad chick on my arm and Ari didn't fall short in the looks area. But, she lacked in personality; her attitude sucked. She was the one to have more enemies than friends.

"I could have met you up there Ari, you act like I'ma run and do something," I spoke into her ear.

"If I were worried about you running off, I'd have you by the arm Kori. I just wasn't going to be trusting these thirsty niggas around my baby." Wrapping her arms around my small waist, she pulled me in for a kiss. Not one for public display of affection, I knew the liquor was hitting. Backing away, I led her to the VIP area before she got me hot and horny.

"Bout damn time you joined us; we ordered 2 bottles," Jada said, grabbing me away from Ari.

"Oh yes, turn up time." Hearing City Girls' *Twerk* come on, I hopped up, giving my girls a show of how well I'd learned to twerk in the last few weeks. Ari looked on with a smug look on her face once she realized all eyes were on me. Closing my eyes, I decided to zone her out and continued bouncing my ass to the beat until I was snatched up.

"Why you always gotta show your ass Kori?" Ari asked, grabbing a hold of my arm. Snatching it back, sucking my teeth and rolling my eyes, I had had enough of her and we had only been at the club for an hour.

"You not going to be roughing my sister up in here, so if your ass got a problem, then you might wanna take your insecure ass home," Kristen warned Ari. Kristen was my older sister by 5 years; she stood in the place of my mom when she walked out on us as kids, leaving us with our grandmother one weekend. So, when Kristen became overprotective, I knew to not question her motives.

"I'm okay," I reassured Kristen, calming her down. Glaring at Ari, I asked, "Can we speak?" while I walked off with her in tow. I stopped at the bathroom, trying to be out of the way. "You see why I don't invite you out Ari, like what the fuck? I'm dancing, having a good time and you fucking up my mood." I crossed my arms across my chest.

"You shaking ya ass all in front of them niggas. I can handle a bitch, but what I can't do is handle a dude, so I ain't with the shit."

Vexed, I replied, "Am I with you or am I with them? Last I checked, I'm with your ass every damn night getting my pussy ate from you or am I bugging Ari?" Shouting above a whisper, I locked eyes with him. The tantalizing trance he had me under had me ignoring every word Ari said. Licking his juicy pink lips, he shook his head in my direction.

"Did you hear me, Kori? I'm out and you're going with me."

Pulling my arm back, I shouted, "No, I'm not! This is my celebration. If you're leaving, I'll meet you home!" Throwing up my hands, I stomped off, hoping she would follow behind me. Turning to look at her, she threw up her hand and walked towards the exit. Sighing, I wasn't going to let her ruin yet another night of fun, so I took the opportunity to look for the guy who held my attention. Unable to find him, I headed back to VIP with my girls. "She left."

"Good, cuz she was aggravating my damn nerves acting like you fucking someone else in this bitch," Kristen stressed. "Have another drink and turn up mami."

Handing me a cup of Hennessy, I spotted ol boy across the way in the other section. Locking eyes with his, I felt shivers run through my body. Turning my gaze away first this time, I felt if I continued to stare at him, I would somehow find my way over to him.

"Chica, who has your attention?" Jada asked, following my gaze. "Ohh, he fine girl, but don't you like that scissor shit you and Ari be doing?"

Chuckling, I playfully slapped her arm. "Shut up Jada. Besides, I'd just want him to eat me out, nothing more."

"That's cute and all boo but, if he eating it, he definitely fucking."

Shrugging, I dismissed the thought. Jada had been my girl since we were kids. Growing up in the same neighborhood and attending the same public school, we grew close. Jada came from two-parent household and her parents loved me and Kristen as if we were theirs. When my grandmother would kick me out for being too grown, I would just go right over to Jada's house for a few days.

"Not all dudes want to just fuck Jada," I tried convincing myself.

"Shut yo old virgin ass up!" I had been with one dude in my life, Amad, but the minute he whipped out his big dick, I called off the sex and broke up with him the same night. I wasn't about that life; I did enjoy getting oral from him tho. Meeting Ari at the age of 22, I was hot, horny and annoyed so, the night she stopped me for making an illegal U-Turn approaching my car, she was taken aback at my beauty. We flirted a little, exchanged numbers and, years later, she was still trying to tell me what I could and couldn't do.

Signaling to my girls that I was ready to leave and find a diner to eat, they followed suite. Rolling down the window, Kristen noticed a dude in a black Range taking up a space in front of the diner. "Excuse me, are you taking this spot?" she asked.

Turning around, I instantly froze, not breaking my stare. Lightly tapping Kristen from the passenger seat, I didn't want her to make it hot. "Let's just find another spot Kris," I suggested.

"No, my feet hurt, so this is going to have to do."

"Yea, don't you see my car here or your ass that blind you don't see me," he boasted.

"Yea, I see you, your ass taking up a spot cuz your thirsty ass posted up outside the diner looking for a bitch to take back to the telly to fuck?!" Kristen spewed. His homeboys started laughing, causing his jaws to clinch as he walked over to the car.

"Let me tell your bougie ass something. I don't know who the fuck you think you talking to, but you and your bird friends need to carry your asses on." He pointed away from him.

Kristen grabbed the door, trying to exit. Pulling her back, I said, "Listen Kristen, it's not worth it." I knew the temper my sister had, so I knew there was only a matter of time before she would go off.

"You know what playboy, I'ma let you have that cuz you think somebody scared." Pressing down on the gas, she almost hit the dude as he jogged to where his car was.

"Fucking bitch!" he spat. Jada and Kristen starting laughing, but I didn't find anything funny.

"You know that was ol boy from the club, right?" Jada asked.

I shook my head and exited the car. By the time we reached the diner, he and his crew were nowhere to be found. Relieved, I entered the diner first and there he was walking in my direction, invading my space. "You see something you like?" he asked in a cocky manner. Rolling my eyes, I brushed past him to where my girls were seated.

"What was that about Kori?" Kristen asked.

"I don't know, but he's been giving me some vibes that I never felt before, maybe I'm just super horny." I shrugged.

"Oh, somebody finally want a taste of some dick huh, you growing up mami," she joked.

Flipping her the bird, I looked over the menu, trying to avoid the hole that was burning on my forehead. Looking up, I caught a glimpse of him in the light. He was a caramel complexion, medium built, full beard, and sported a low Cesar cut complemented by a mole on the ridge of his nose. Blushing, I flashed him a sexy smile and looked back down at the menu. Feeling the shock shoot to my kitty, I crossed my legs tightly, trying to suppress the urge that went through my body. Jada lightly kicked me from the under the table, catching my attention. "What?!" I peeked over at the smug look on Kristen's face.

"You drooling over that rude ass nigga?"

Rolling my eyes, I ordered and ate my food while thinking about this dude. Feeling my phone vibrate, I looked at it, noticing I had a few missed calls and texts from Ari, which I happily dismissed. "Ladies, I gotta get home. Ari blowing me up and I'm not trying to be fighting tonight." Paying the bill, I walked outside while they used the restroom.

"Aye mami, let me holla at you?" Before I could answer, he was in my personal space, taking in my scent.

"Apparently, I don't have a choice now, do I?" Cocking my head to the side, I blushed, displaying my dimple.

"I'm saying, I may not be your type but I see you been eyeing me, so that tells me you're interested."

Waving him off, I replied, "Boy, if you don't get."

His jaws clenched. "Ain't nothing little boy over here," he cockily said.

Rolling my eyes, I tried walking around him until he pulled me in to his embrace. "For real ma, just gimme a chance to take you out."

Removing his hands from my waist, I said, "I'm good playa." I looked over at Kristen talking to this tall dark skinned dude while Jada went to get the car.

"So, did you give him your number?" Jada questioned.

"Why would I, Jada? I have a woman at home!"

"If you say so." Kristen walked her happy ass back to the car and we left.

Chapter 2

Edo

I entered my condo. "Yo Diesel, shorty gave you her number?" he asked.

"Yea, told you stop trying to holla at that gay chick." He shrugged.

"Nigga, fuck you. She only gay cuz she ain't had a real nigga to lock her down. I'ma eat her pussy so good, she ain't gonna know who that bitch she was with is!" I boasted.

Chuckling, Diesel gave up. I was his right-hand man and he knew my ass could be persistent when it came to the broads I wanted. Grabbing the stacks of money from the duffle bag, I set up the money counter. "It's been a good week if I must say so myself," I reminded Diesel as he cut open the blunt.

"Yea, cuz I had to run down on them boys from 3rd avenue," Diesel said out of anger. "They keep playing with me, I'ma have to make an example outta one of em."

Shaking my head, I said, "I told you , you keep letting them slide so they see that shit as a weakness. Besides, just tell Unc. He will take care of it, so your pretty little hands don't get dirty." I laughed, throwing a few stacks in Diesel's direction.

"Nigga, fuck you," Diesel spewed, taking a toke from the blunt.

Diesel and I had been working for his uncle Deuce since we were 15 and 17 years old. We started off as runners until Diesel's near death experience, and Deuce decided to pull us and had us overseeing four of the blocks from 3rd 149th to 161st Street in the Bronx. That was over 10 years ago and we had gradually moved up on the ladder. Deuce was ready to retire with his wife and live the stress free life but, until he felt like I was ready to take over the organization, he had to keep his feet wet.

Deuce raised me from the age of 10 when my sister died in a car accident, and I soon met Diesel after he moved up from Virginia. Diesel, being a southern boy, no one took a liking to him. One day, he was getting jumped in the playground. I jumped in, sealing the deal to our friendship.

"But yo, I think I'ma invite shorty out this week. You want me to see if she'll bring that lil thick joint along?" Diesel quizzed.

"Bet, set that shit up." Grabbing my stacks, I headed to my bedroom, leaving Diesel in my man cave for the night.

Diesel sent a text to Kristen.

Diesel: aye ma, I'm trying to see you one day this week, wassup?

Kristen: that sounds like a plan, just give me a time and place and I'm there

Diesel: aight bet but you gotta bring ya homegirl along for my boy

Kristen: my homegirl who the dark skinned one?

Diesel: nah the thick one

Kristen: oh my sister, aight even tho she will turn it down

Diesel: c'mon ma make it work, we just wanna chill

Kristen: okay I'll beg her, but you owe me

Diesel: say no more

Diesel ended the convo and got himself comfortable on my couch; it wasn't no way he was driving home after the long night he had.

Chapter 3

Kori

"Kori, answer ya damn phone," Ari said, tossing my iPhone in my direction as I peacefully slept.

Rolling my eyes, I felt the vibration going off for the past few minutes. I was lucky that Ari hadn't answered it after all the fighting we had done the night before. "Seriously Ari, you gon throw my phone at me? I swear, you're trying my patience," I stressed, picking up the call.

"Hey mami, I know you're not still sleep. It's damn near 12pm Kori!"

"Kristen, I realize that, but we did get it after 5am-," Before I could finish my sentence, Ari was sucking her teeth and mumbling something under her breath. Ignoring her cries for attention, I asked, "What's so urgent?"

"I know you're going to probably say no but-"

If Kristen started off a saying like that, it was more than likely something off the wall she wanted me to do. "Can you go on a double date with me pretty please?" she begged.

"Kristen seriously, no. Take Jada with you damn." Rolling my eyes, I knew I shouldn't have answered this damn phone.

"Jada can't come, remember she's going out of state to visit her family this week? So, that leaves you and I can't go on no double date alone."

Sighing, I replied, "I'll think about it. When is this happening?" Getting up from the bed, I headed to the kitchen to make a cup of tea for this killer migraine.

"I'll text you the details but more than likely Thursday night, since I know Ari will be working late," she reassured.

"Okay but you know I work til 5, so y'all gon have to come get me after, if I decide to go."

"See, you're the best little sister."

Before I could tell her it was a definite answer, she hung up. Smiling at my phone, I was greeted with Ari's smug look once I looked up. "Is there a problem?"

"Yea, there is. Where the fuck you went til 5am Kori? The club closes at 3," she questioned, walking into my person space. Seeing her seethe, I knew she wanted to have yet another argument.

"I went to get food Ari. Stop being so insecure; it's such a damn turn off," I spat, trying to move around her.

Ari pinned me against the island. "Nah, if you weren't doing nothing foul, let me smell ya pussy Kori!"

Looking as if she had lost her mind, I was taken back. "Ari, I'm not doing this with you." Lifting my body up off of the island, Ari backhanded me across my face.

"I said let me smell ya pussy, since you ain't doing no foul shit. Why you fighting it?!" she spat, looking me in my face.

Trying to hold back the tears, I touched the stinging on my face as Ari lifted my leg and stuck her finger in my pussy. Wincing in pain, I watched as she smelled it. "You better stop playing with me, Kori. I will kill you before I let you play me," she chastised as she left the kitchen.

Once she was gone, I let the tears fall. Holding in my cries, I vowed I'd never let her see me shed another tear. Picking up my phone, I texted

Kristen that I was down to double date. After wiping my face, I retrieved to the room, only to find that Ari was in the shower. Packing up the few items she had at my apartment, she had to get out and fast before I ended up on *Fatal Attraction* or *Snapped*. Throwing on a tee and sweats, I started tossing bags down the stairs at the front door.

"Yo, what the fuck you doing Kori?"

"What does it look like Ari? I'm breaking up with you. I'm not about to keep taking any more of your shit. The insecurities is one thing, but now you fucking sticking your fingers in my pussy to see if I'm cheating and putting your hands on me!" I shouted, walking in her direction.

"You bugging out Kori, relax and let's talk about this shit," she tried to reassure me, but I was so far gone; I just needed her out.

"Ari, get out before I call your captain and have you arrested for domestic violence, you bipolar bitch" I spat. Ari charged in my direction, wrapping her hands around my throat. Being smaller in size, I started swinging my legs, kicking her until she loosened her grip on my neck. Coughing and holding my neck, I had to get away from her and fast or she was going to do something stupid.

Getting up from the floor, I rushed out of the bedroom into one of my spare bedrooms. Closing and locking the door, I cursed myself for not bringing my phone with me.

"Kori, open the fucking door!" Ari shouted, kicking the door.

"Ari, just go, we can talk about this later," I pleaded through sobs. Hearing the constant kicking and banging, I realized Ari had her gun on her.

"Kori, I told you I will kill you before I let your ass walk away from me!"

Feeling the vibration on my arm, I was happy I didn't take off my Apple Watch last night. Kristen's name lit up, calming me down a little. "Ari, please just go," I kept begging her while answering the call. Turning the volume down on my end so she wouldn't know, Ari kept bagging on the door with her gun.

"Koriann, open the fucking door or I'm going to shoot right through this bitch."

"Please Ari, just calm down, it doesn't have to end like this. Just go your way and I'll go mine."

They say to always take heed to your woman's intuition, right? I let my guard down and decided to fight the feelings in my gut and look how this all played out.

The gun went off, causing me to scream in an agonizing panic. Ari backed up, looking at the damage to the bedroom door before fleeing my condo. Not checking to see if the bullet hit me or not, she was gone.

Chapter 4

Kristen

Hearing my sister cry out in horror, I hurried up and got dressed, texting Diesel so he could meet me over there. I wasn't going to be no fool and show up over there with no back up, in case Ari wanted to act stupid.

"Can you drive faster Edo, damn!" I cursed him out. "That bitch is crazy and, if she hurt my sister, I'm going to jail today!" I boasted from the back seat.

"Calm ya ass down Kristen, we not about to let that shit happen," Diesel assured me.

Listening to my phone on speaker, we heard the skid of Ari's car as we were nearing Kori's complex. As my heart raced, all I could think of was my little sister's wellbeing. The shuffling in the background and the screams scared me shitless. Edo started driving at 80 mph until we were right in front of her building.

Hopping out of the car, not caring if they followed or not, I had to get to Kori's apartment. With Edo and Diesel in tow, we climbed to the 3rd floor apartment where her door was slightly ajar. There were a few neighbors hovering around on the floor. "She left, she ran outta here so fast," one of them said.

"Who?" Diesel asked

"The tall one, the girlfriend."

Rushing into the apartment, I found Kori in one of her guest rooms up against the wall crying. Looking at the damage, I saw the bullet lodged into the wall just above her head.

"She, she tried to kill me," Kori spoke in almost a whisper.

Edo scooped a shaken Kori up. "Yo, grab her purse and phone. We gotta get her outta here before that looney bitch come back." Locking up her apartment, we went to the car.

"I'll drive her car," Diesel suggested. "You go with Edo, I'll just follow."

Running behind Edo, I hopped in the backseat with Kori, holding her as she sat in silence. Not knowing what was going through her mind or where to take her, Edo suggested we lay low in his house because Ari would for sure be coming by my house in search for her.

"You sure? We could always check in a hotel," I quipped.

"Don't insult me like that. That's my wifey right there, so y'all staying with me," he said, looking in the mirror at me.

Defeated, I didn't protest. "Okay," I said, bringing Kori close to me. It had been years since I had to play mommy and be Kori's backbone. When my mother dropped us off to our grandmother's house, I didn't know she wouldn't be returning. She didn't leave a note, no phone call, not even as much as an I love you. Kori took it hard for a month straight; she cried for mami and she never came back for us. It was at this very moment where I felt like the helpless 10 year old consoling a crying 5 year old Koriann.

Pulling up to a huge house, I looked on in admiration. Looking down at Kori, I shook her awake. Startling her, Kori jumped, kicking the back of Edo's chair and crying. "She's going to kill me, Kris; abuela can't handle that. What if she visits her?" Kori asked, rambling on.

"It's going to be fine; I'ma send someone to watch your grandmother's house. You're good shorty." Edo pulled Kori in, escorting her to the house with me following closely behind them. "C'mon, come take a shower ma," Edo instructed Kori.

"Diesel should be right behind us, make yourself comfortable. I'll handle your sister."

Kori turned around in a panic. "No! She comes with me, please." Showing us the bathroom and giving her a change of clothes, I sat with Kori while she cleaned up.

Chapter 5

Edo

I know it may look crazy bringing a chick to my crib that I knew nothing about but, hearing her panic and watching the fright on her face, I acted on emotion and felt like I had to protect her at any cost. Out of all the women I dated, none of them knew where I laid my head; I had spots for that kind of activity. Something about Kori was different; her aura drew me in. Entering the den, I saw the look on Diesel's face.

"So, you letting shorty stay here? Cuz if so, we gon all shack up here til this shit blows over."

Rubbing my hand across my goatee, I was stumped.

"What you think Paris gon say when you start ducking her calls?" Forgetting about my on again off again girl led me to realize I had to make her a thing of the past.
"You know this some fucked up shit, you being captain save a hoe and you got a shorty already," Diesel chuckled.

"Yea, I know but you know Paris is just somebody to fuck with; she ain't nobody I'm trying to wife," I said, trying to convince myself.

Paris was a chick I met 2 years ago in the mall. Her card had declined when she checked out. Pissed off, I cursed her ass out because she had me on the line for more than I anticipated for her card to had declined. After seeing the look of defeat, plus the pampers and bottles, I couldn't let this mother just leave like that.

So, after purchasing her items, she asked how she could repay me. Looking over her with hungry eyes, I knew exactly what she could do. One hook up led to me and her shacking up a couple of days out the week while her baby father's family helped out. The thing with Paris was she didn't want to work or go to school. Hell, half the time, I had to remind her to go see her child.

Paris was 30 and maturing with age was an understatement for her. Between her partying ways and always having her hand out for money, I had grown tired of taking care of her.

"Edo, why haven't I seen you in a while? Who is that bitch you with? So, her pussy must be made of gold huh?" I could hear her now.

Grabbing up my phone, I sent her a text, letting her know I would be coming through for a few; Kori needed the rest anyway. Letting Diesel know what was up, I told him when I got back, we would have to take them shopping. He nodded and told me don't come back fucked up. Chuckling, I knew Paris would be pissed and ready to fight. Shaking my head, I grabbed up some food for her and Parnell; I was sure she didn't get her lazy ass up to cook.

I had Paris staying in a 2 bedroom on 211 and White Plains Road, which gave me the opportunity to get away with shit. She had caught me on numerous occasions with bitches and stayed around, hoping I would change, but hell had to freeze over before I committed to her.

"Sup shorty." She jumped up from the couch, ready to argue as usual.

"Where the fuck you been Edo?" Tapping her feet with her arms folded across her chest, she continued, "Oh wait, let me guess, you been fucking around on me, huh?"

Walking up on me and mushing my head, I constantly reminded Paris of keeping her hands to herself; she seemed to never learn. I wouldn't hit a chick, but I damn sure would shake the shit out of her. "Man, fuck all that bullshit you talking about. Where your son bitch?" I questioned, looking around at the quiet apartment.

Rolling her eyes, she replied, "With his grandmother, why?"

Stepping over the toys scattered about the living room, I made a mistake stopping by. "He's always at his grandmother's; when the fuck you gon be a mother, Paris?" Agitated, I kicked a toy truck across the floor. Dropping the bag of food on the end table, I headed straight to the bedroom.

"I sent him over there, so we could have some alone time Edo," she protested, following behind me.

"I ain't trying to hear that shit. You be having shorty over there all the time; then, you wonder why I never wife ya ass." Tossing the white tee I had on and stripping of the jeans I had on, my dick print showed through the boxers. "Since ya ass want some alone time, come show me what that mouth do then, Paris," I demanded.

Like the good girl she was, she cat walked over to me, dropping to her knees. Removing my semi erect dick out of my boxers, she grabbed the shaft. "Is this why you agitated daddy? You been missing my lips wrapped around ya dick?"

Rolling my eyes to the ceiling, I said, "Shut up and just suck this shit P." Pushing her head on my dick, I ordered, "Open that mouth wide."

Doing as she was told, I fucked her face. "And I dare you to gag, you got all that mouth, right."

Paris was a pro in the dick sucking area. Removing my dick from her mouth, she licked up and down my shaft, gently squeezing the top. Going down to my balls, Paris gently sucked on them while she jerked my shaft. Feeling the precum slide down my dick, Paris wrapped her lips around my dick and bobbed her head up and down on my shit until she felt my dick jerk a little.

Catching myself moaning, "Shit," I held her head, still fucking her mouth. "I'm bout to cum, you better swallow all this shit baby." Between the slurping and Paris' moans, I busted right down her throat. Watching her swallow all my seeds, I was drained. Holding the dresser nearby for balance, Paris got up.

"I know you gon give me some dick, right?"

Walking around her to the bathroom, "Nah, you good shorty," I stated matter of factly.

"The fuck you mean Eladio? You just came to get your dick sucked, you could of had that bitch that you been with sucking ya funky ass dick!" she shouted.

37

Pushing Paris out of the bathroom and locking the door, I stepped in the shower. "She is not about to ruin my mood," I mumbled to no one in particular. Hearing my phone ring from the other side of the door, I cursed myself for being so damn careless. "If this bitch touch my phone, lord forgive me." Thinking about what phone I brought in from the car, I realized it was my work phone.

"Diesel is calling you, should I answer it?"

"Paris, if you pick up my phone, I'ma snap your neck," I huffed. "I gotta get outta this bitch before she make me kill her dumb ass."

Taking a quick shower, I emerged from the bathroom. Grabbing a sweat suit and my phone, I hurried and got dressed. Finding Paris on the couch flicking through channels on the tv, she looked up at me and rolled her eyes

"Fuck wrong with ya dumb ass?!" Already knowing the answer, I taunted her.

"Fuck you, Edo; you might as well go live with the bitch."

Stopping in my tracks, "I just might, that don't sound half bad," I retorted.

Chuckling, she tossed the remote in my direction, almost hitting me in my head. "If that shit would of hit me, you would of been sorry." Slamming the door behind me, I hopped in my Range.

Chapter 6

Ari

Rushing out of Kori's condo, I didn't know where I was headed, but I knew I had to get ghost and fast. Pulling out of her driveway, I headed straight to my partner's house. Banging on his door, I knew he would be pissed that I showed up unannounced, but fuck it. "Raj, open up! I fucked up this time!" I shouted.

"Yo, what the fuck Ari? You out here acting like somebody coming for you." He rushed me in his apartment, slamming his door shut.

Pacing the floor, I stammered, "Yo, I shot inside of Kori's apartment. I don't know if I hit her or not; I got outta there so quick after I heard her scream cuz I knew her neighbors were calling the cops."

"You did what? Have you checked on her and when the hell did this happen?"

Sitting down on his sofa trying to remain calm, I jumped back up, pumping my fist in the air "Yo, if she got hit, you know I'm fucked right? Captain said I had one more chance," I stressed.

"Listen baby, calm down." Raj pulled me in for a bear hug and I broke down.

"I love her, but she be trying me; she makes me act up," I sighed.

"Ari I told you them girls will drive you crazy, but you don't be thinking," he said, dismissing my tears. "Kori young, fine, educated and she got the body that most of these bitches pay for, so dealing with her is going to bring you a lot of stress but you just had to get a taste of her huh?" Raj chuckled.

Playfully slapping his arm, I replied, "You just mad cuz I don't share her."

He thought for a minute. "You damn right, we done shared all your bitches except her. What's so special about this one, huh?"

"You wouldn't believe me if I told you." Shrugging, I entered the kitchen to pour me a drink.

Try me," he challenged.

"She's a virgin, dated a dude but never fucked, so I turned her out and she been mine ever since. So no, I'm not sharing her," I stated matter of factly.

Raj had been my partner for the past 8 years on the force. At first, I swore he was an asshole because he would do any and everything in his power to get me pulled in the office, only to find out he just wanted some pussy. The first night we hooked up, we were looking for these 2 dudes who had killed a mother of five. The case was stressing us out and, the minute we caught both of them bastards, we headed right to the bar to celebrate.

After 4 drinks and a few double shots, we ended up at the nearest hotel. Fucking and sucking all night, we woke up feeling like shit. I tried to avoid him as much as possible until he presented the opportunity to have a threesome.

I had never been with a chick but was always curious so, after a shot of Patron and a few pulls from the blunt, I was ready and that chick turned me out. I would never forget Chyna; she was my first experience and we kept fucking with each other for years, until her man found out and she ended up taking her life. In between that, Raj and I shared a bed with about 5 other women, until I met Kori. He wanted me to invite her in so bad but, the minute I found out she was a virgin, I had hit the jackpot. I could continue to fuck Raj and have her without feeling guilty.

"That's fucked up, but I'ma give her a pass cuz she a virgin. But, on some real shit, you gotta reach out to her peoples to see if she good."

Taking his advice, I headed right to her grandmother's house. I knew her sister wouldn't open the door, after trying her number numerous times. Her grandmother was adamant that she hadn't heard from her, so I ain't press the issue any further. Sucking my teeth, I saw that I had a call that I really didn't want to answer. "Yeah," I said dryly

"What you mean yea? You ain't see me call your ass for the past couple of hours, Ari?" he shouted into the phone.

"Listen, I been dealing with some heavy shit. I know you looking for your money and I assure you that I'ma get it to you," I tried reasoning. The phone went silent.

"When Ari? You playing fucking games with me and I'm not about to have you make a fool of me. I'll kill you and feed you to my dogs for dinner; keep fucking with me!" he spat into the phone.

"Ok, ok, that's not necessary; I'll get it to you first thing Friday morning."

I heard him chuckle. "Friday morning and, if 12pm roll around and I don't hear from you, just know I'm coming for everyone you love."

Hearing the beeps, I knew he ended the call. "What the fuck did I get myself into?" I stressed while sitting in my car.

Chapter 7

Kristen

Watching Kori sleep, I decided to go find Diesel and see what he was doing. Noticing the missed calls from my grandmother and Jada, my stomach fell to the pit of my stomach. "Bueno," I said, speaking to my grandmother.

"Where is your sister, Kristen? I've been calling her for hours after that crazy girlfriend of hers left from around here," my grandmother stressed.

"She's not home abuela. She's with me, safe," I tried to reassure her.

"What is going on mija, is she okay?"

Not one to work my grandmother up, I simply told her yes and ended the call. "Wassup heffa, you and your sister in some trouble cuz your grandmother called me frantic?"

"She got into some shit with Ari, but we are good. We are with Diesel and Edo," I assured her.

"Them niggas from the diner?"

"Yea," I sighed, looking around the house for the guys.

"Well, y'all be safe. If I have to catch a flight back to the city, I will," Jada stressed.

"Nah mama, enjoy your vacation. I got her."

Walking around the corner, I heard the front door slam. "Shit," I exclaimed while holding my chest; Edo had scared me.

"Why you creeping around my house?" he fumed.

"I'm not. I was looking for either one of y'all. Kori is sleeping and her ex has been blowing up my phone, so now what?"

"That bitch ain't about to do nothing. You hungry? I'll take y'all to get some food," Edo said.

"Yeah."

"Aight, go wake ya sister so we can get some food and take y'all shopping."

Watching him disappear, I headed straight to Kori. After convincing her that we were safe, she finally got dressed and met us downstairs.

Chapter 8

Diesel

Looking up at Kristen, I knew she was a prize that I had to stick with. Just like her sister, she had a lot going for herself and no kids, which meant no drama. I didn't know why I was playing myself because I had 2 baby mothers and one I still fucked with on and off, so I came with a lot of baggage.

"You okay?" Kristen asked.

"Yea, I'm good, just checking some messages. I'll be in the car in a minute." After she walked away, I returned Rochelle's call, my baby mama from hell. "Yo, what's so fucking urgent?"

"Hold up nigga, I know you not talking to me. I'm not your other baby mama Jewel!" she barked.

Already annoyed, I said, "Listen Rochelle, if this isn't no urgent matter about my son, then get the fuck off my line with all the bullshit!" Slouching my shoulders in defeat, she went on and on about lil Dee needing new sneakers and shit. With as much money as I give her, you would think she would leave me the fuck alone. "Yo Rochelle, I gotta go;

I'll send you some damn money for my son!" Ending the call, I dialed Jewel's number.

"Hey baby."

"Wassup ma, you good?" I asked, trying to read her tone through the phone.

"I'm good. I'm just trying to understand why I haven't heard from you and, when I call, you never answer," she wined.

"Listen ma, I'm handling business and you know how that goes. Soon as it's set, I'm going to link with you; my daughter good?"

"Yea, she's good?"

"Aight bet." Ending the call, I headed to the car. Rochelle was this older chick from the strip club I was fucking with her in high school, thinking I hit the jackpot with a cougar. Her ass ended up pregnant and started milking me for every dime I made. Never wanting to work a real job and me telling her once I got her pregnant that stripping shit was dead, she always felt I had to provide for my son and her. After we split up and I met Jewel, she always held me down, but she was just too damn crazy. Jewel was a spoiled brat and wanted everything her way or no way; she came from a wealthy family so she didn't have to work, but she also had to hide me. Her parents didn't approve of her dating any thugs, so I never met them. They believed Jewel when she said that me and her were only a one-night stand, so she could continue to reap their monetary benefits.

"Y'all ready to go?"

"Yea, we was waiting on you," Kris answered. Hopping in the car, I pulled her in for an embrace and felt a relief from life.

Chapter 9

Kori

I couldn't have asked for a better damn Saturday if you asked me. From walking in from the club, I should have told Ari to leave. Then, she hit me and shot at me. Now, I was here in fucking hiding cuz the bitch was crazy. She had blew up my phone so much, I ended up blocking her number, her partner, and her house number. I knew leaving Ari was going to be an issue, but I never imagined it would be because she shot at me. Instead of her checking to see if I was hit, she ran like a coward.

"So, what's your favorite store?" Edo asked, drawing me out of my thoughts.

"Neiman Marcus," I responded while looking back out the window. He placed his hand on my thigh. The fire I felt shot through me, instantly getting me hot. Smiling over at him flirtatiously, I laid back and got comfortable. Looking in the rearview, I saw that Kristen and Diesel were knocked out.

"What's on your mind?"

"Just everything that happened today. How long am I supposed to be hidden Edo?" I asked.

"Call me Eladio, ma, and yea I know this shit is crazy but I'm trying to keep you outta harm's way."

Raising my eyebrow, I was lost. "What you mean harm's way? Ari isn't going to really shoot me, Eladio; she's just trying to scare me," I tried to reassure him.

"Whatever the case may be, I'm still keeping you safe. She already shot at you, who knows when a woman is scorn," he stated flatly.

"You don't know that."

Squeezing my thigh, he said, "Just trust me, Kori, and take a leave from work, it's for the best right now."

Rolling my eyes, I just wanted to shop and forget about the day's events. After shopping for hours, we ended up at Del Frisco's Steakhouse. Kristen was beaming with this glow from flirting with Diesel. "You good ma?" Edo asked.

"Yes, stop asking me that," I chuckled.

"I'm just saying, you sitting over there all quiet. Come sit on my lap." He pulled out his chair, patting his lap.

"Boy bye, we are in a public place," I blushed.

Grabbing my hand, he pulled me over to him, causing me to display my dimples. "See, if you ain't feeling me, why I got you looking all goofy?"

Playfully slapping his arm away, I got up from his lap, ready to go. Looking over at him, I had to admit being that close to him had me ready to test the waters and get dicked down, but I was sure he came with a lot of issues. He was handsome and paid, so I knew he had a woman or a bunch of kids running through New York.

After returning home, Diesel and Kristen disappeared into the room she was occupying. "You want something to drink?" Edo asked, pouring himself a glass of Hennessy.

"Sure." What did I have to lose? Being tipsy around this handsome specimen shouldn't be too bad. Passing me the full glass of Hennessy straight, Edo told me a little about him and, when I revealed to him that I had never been with a man, he almost spit out his drink.

"Yo, you serious ma?!" he choked.

"Yea, I mean I am, well, I was dating a female," I chuckled, looking at the bewildered look on his face. "Fix your face," I laughed.

"So, how old are you ma?" he questioned.

"26, why you ask?"

"So, you mean to tell me you ain't never had no dick and you 26? Nah, you bugging." He got up and walked around the island, coming to sit beside me.

"I'm serious, I never felt the urge to try it out."

Lifting me from the seat, he spun me around. "So, all this ass is just natural. Ain't no nigga give you no back shots?"

Falling over laughing at his remark, I rolled my eyes and said, "You are so crazy but, nah, I'm serious."

"So, she fucked you with a strap?"

"No boy, move. I've only used toys on myself." Walking around Edo, I saw the look of lust in his eyes. I drank some more Henny to calm my nerves down, but all it did was make me horny.

Pulling me into his legs, Edo kissed my lips. Accepting his advances, I let a soft moan escape my lips. As we hungrily kissed each other, Edo picked me up and carried me to the master bedroom. "Umm," I said out of anticipation, "don't be rough." I warned him.

Lying me on the bed, he said, "I'ma be gentle, I promise."

Not sure if this was how I wanted to lose my virginity, there was no turning back now. Pulling off my jeans, I removed my shirt and bra. Opening my legs to take him in, Edo kissed my lips and my neck, stopping at my breasts as his tongue circled my hard nipples. Throwing my head back in ecstasy, my eyes rolled in the back of my head. Grabbing both breasts, he kissed from one to the other, kissed down to my kitty. Sliding my wet thong to the side, he blew on my pussy.

"Oh, my gawd," I said, damn near choking myself.

"You been missing out ma, but daddy gon show you," Edo said while I looked down at him with lustful eyes. "You ready?!"

Looking at him as if he was crazy, "If you don't fuck me, Edo, I will take the dick," I purred. Feeling his lips on my pussy made me go into overdrive "Umm yes, eat that shit."

Edo opened my lips and began sucking and licking on my clit. "Shit, I'm going to cum Edo." Moving to his rhythm, I felt myself creaming, but he wasn't done yet; he continued to please me. Trying to run away, Edo pulled me back towards him, crying out in pleasure. "Edo please, stop ssss," I said while throwing my head back.

"You sure you want me to stop?" he asked with my juices coating his beard.

"No Edo, don't stop, I'm going to cum again." Sticking his finger inside of me, I begged, "Shit Edo, fuck me please!"

Taking his dick out, he asked, "You ready for this ma?"

Unsure but full of bliss, I nodded my head. Slowly working the head of his dick in, I felt my kitty ripping. "Fuck," I moaned. Inching further in, Edo massaged my clit with one hand. "Umm I'ma cum, I'ma cum baby." Just as I was squirting, Edo pushed his dick all the way in, breaking me in. "Arghh!" I shouted out in pain and ecstasy. He stroked me until my orgasm subsided. Pulling out while still hard, I saw the little bit of blood coated on him.

Embarrassed, I jumped up, running to the bathroom. Hearing Edo laugh, he said, "You good ma, c'mon open the door." He tapped on it lightly.

Grabbing the tissue to wipe me, it stung. "Wait," I pleaded.

"Just run a shower, I'ma get in with you. Your little tight pussy gon be sore for a bit."

"Edo, it's not funny," I cried out. Unlocking the door, I had tears in my eyes.

"C'mon ma, I already knew you was a virgin so stop beating yourself up; this shit is normal," he said.

Cocking my head to the side, I replied, "Not at this age, it's not normal." He just found the whole ordeal funny, which pissed me off even more. After showering, Edo suggest we lay up until the morning.

"You trust me, right ma?"

Looking up at him, I answered, "Yea, just don't get me caught up!" What the fuck was I thinking at this moment? I had just had the best orgasm in my life, Edo didn't press me about fucking him, and Ari had tried to kill me so, with that, I fell asleep in Edo's arms.

Chapter 10

Edo

Hearing my phone vibrating back to back, I knew it was urgent because it was my work line. Looking down at the caller, it was my uncle trying to get in touch with me. "Fuck," I whispered. Looking over at Kori, I slid from under her as she stirred in her sleep. Smiling at her, I picked up my phone. "Yo boss man, sorry."

"Nigga, I know the reason you not answering my calls better not lead to you laying in some pussy."

Sucking my teeth, I retorted, "Unc nah, I had another situation I had to handle, but what's the word?"

"Yea, well Diesel ass must be taking care of the same shit cuz I can't get in touch with his black ass either!" Deuce barked.

"Yea, it's crazy on this end," I stressed, trying to change the subject.

"Anyway, I'ma need you to pay somebody a visit for me next week. I'll give you the details in person; I'm not trying to do too much talking on the phone."

"Aight, say no more." Walking out of the room, I heard Kristen's screams of pleasure and knew my boy was killing her shit.

"How the blocks looking?"

"They aight, had to run up on a few of the young boys who was trying to play with us."

"Right right, aight so yea I'ma hit you in a few days with the job I got for you." I nodded my head "And you better answer when I call nigga!" he demanded.

"Copy that." Ending the call, I headed back to the room.

Entering, I saw Kori gathering her clothes off the chair. "Wassup ma, where you going?"

"To my room. Apparently, you have a chick and tonight was just a mistake," she said, brushing passed me.

Trying to grab her arm, she stormed down the stairs. "Kori, it's not like that!" I yelled after her.

"Typical nigga shit, so what the fuck is it like Eladio!" she said, putting emphasis on my name.

Chasing after her, I replied, "That was business ma," while swatting her arm.

"At 1am Edo, do I look fucking stupid to you?" Crossing her arms and tapping her feet impatient, I knew I had to give her some proof. "Fuck this, I'm going back home. I don't have time for this shit!" she started yelling.

Placing my hand over her mouth to shut her up, I displayed my phone call log that said Unc. Looking at her expression soften, I said while smiling, "See, so come back to lay with big daddy, wifey."

"Whatever Eladio, you ain't shit" she said, heading back to the room.

The next couple of days, I was back and forth between my house and Paris' crib. "I see you found your way back over here," Paris said, rolling her eyes as I walked through the door.

"You just can't appreciate a nigga presence, huh? You gotta say shit every damn time!" I fumed. Looking over at Parnell playing with his toys, I scooped him up. "Sup lil man, what you over here doing?"

"Playing, can I come hang with you Edo?" he asked.

"Yea, lil man," I said grabbing him an outfit. I figured I'd take him to the mall.

I called up Diesel to bring his two kids along; it'd been a minute since we weren't working. "Yo, who you got at the house with the girls?" Diesel asked.

"I got Sean and Eric there watching my crib and Chris looking over her grandmother's house," I stressed.

"Don't you think you should tell Unc what's going on before her girl put us and our organization in jeopardy?"

Thinking about what Diesel just said, it could blow up in my face hiding out a female in my crib. But, I also didn't want him to think I was letting pussy run my life, like he claimed on many occasions from my dealings with Paris.

Chapter 11

Deuce

"Baby, don't stress them grown men," Marie said, rubbing my shoulders. "You will give yourself a heart attack trying to keep up with their dealings outside of the game," she tried to assure me.

"I hear what you saying but, if something happens to Edo because he wasn't on top of his A-game, I can't step down!" I had been thinking about stepping down for a few months; I wasn't as quipped and young as I looked. I had been in the streets since I was 14 and, at the age of 54, I was ready to put it behind him and settle down with my wife of 20 years.

Coming from a poor family, I wanted different for myself. After being teased about my clothes being dirty and not having the latest fashion, I ran into one of the older dudes on the block Bo, who took me under the wing. Bo taught me the game and told me to always be a step ahead of everyone. What Bo didn't tell me was to have a legit hustle on the side because when Bo got knocked, he had nothing to fall back on.

"C'mon, come lay down with me, babe," Marie cooed, falling back into the king bed.

Looking over at my wife, I had to agree that I was one of the luckiest men alive. Marie was 48 and didn't look a day over 35; she was a caramel complexion with honey colored eyes, curly auburn hair, standing at 5'5. Marie had a coke bottle shape, inherited from her black father. She had the best of both worlds, Puerto Rican and Black. Marie was raised by her single mother; she was what you would call the bad seed. If her mother said go right, she went left and, when she met me, she was running from an abusive ex.

"Aight ma, you gon look out for daddy?" I asked, pulling Marie down to the end of the bed.

"Anything to get you in the bed with me, pa," Marie purred in my ear.

We made love all afternoon, and the ringing of my phone stopped our cuddling session. "Yo," I said in a hoarse voice.

"Yo Deuce, ol girl came around here trying to purchase some product."

I clinched my jaws. "And what happened?" I barked. "I hope none of you niggas sold her anything?"

"Jeff said he wasn't about to front her no work, but Issac did," Mark said.

"You mean to tell me she owe me money and y'all dum niggas still frontin this bitch money!" Vexed, I got up from the bed, grabbing my robe. "Find her and bring her to me and, if I see that you can't deliver Mark, you gon wish you would have killed Issac!" I spat, ending the call.

"Is everything okay baby?" Marie asked, concerned.

"Nothing I can't handle, so take your pretty little self back to sleep," I assured her. "I gotta go to the city. I'll be back tomorrow." Kissing her and leaving out the room, I knew I had to remind Ari that I wasn't the one to play with. I couldn't risk losing everything I worked for, including the record company I invested in years ago: Diamond Records.

Chapter 12

Kori

After calling Edo for the past few hours, I was not going to stay in this house bored out my mind. I had called off work for the week with the flu. Between my grandmother calling me every day and wondering where Ari was, I was suffering with cabin fever. Unlike myself, Kristen was allowed to leave the house, but they were scared I'd go back to Ari.

"Hey boo," Jada sang into the phone.

"Hey ma, wassup with you?"

"Ain't shit, I'll be home soon. I miss you!" she confessed.

"Same here boo, I'm tired of sitting in this house not doing anything," I stressed with agitation.

"Yea, I get that but, if Kristen says it's for the best, then I say just use this time to relax," Jada tried reasoning.

"I guess." After wrapping up the phone call with Jada, I called my grandmother.

"Hola mija, are you okay?"

"Yes abuela, I am. I'm just going through something," I tried to convince her.

"Like what, when have you kept a secret from me?" she asked.

"I'm not hiding anything-"

Cutting me off, she said, "Bullshit Koriann, there is someone outside of my house watching it. Are you in any danger? Is it that girlfriend of yours because she paid me a visit?" She rambled off.

"No grandma, I have someone watching the house because I heard that there were a few break-ins in your neighborhood mama." I hated lying to her but, if I had told her the truth, it would surely worry her.

"Oh I see, I didn't hear about that," she said sarcastically.

"Yes but, mama, I'm going to let you go. I'll call you tomorrow."

"Okay mija, love you."

"Love you too, mama." Ending the call, I felt like shit having to keep secrets from her, but I wanted to protect my grandmother at any cost. She was 70 and didn't need the extra stress of Ari and my drama. Unblocking Ari's number, I was ready to face her and see what she had to say for her actions.

Hearing the door unlocking, I contemplating looking over my shoulder; it seemed like Edo took my virginity then disappeared.

"Wassup wifey." He walked up on me, pulling me into his embrace.

Rolling my eyes, I eased off of him. "I'm not in the mood for you, Edo," I spat.

"C'mon now, what's the attitude for? You want me to dick you down again?"

Pushing past him, I answered, "No, I don't. I want to leave and go home." I stomped off in the direction of the bedroom.

"Kori, you know you can't leave until we see what Ari's motives are!" he shouted.

"Wrong, I know what her motives are and they aren't to kill me. You don't know her, so stop acting like you do," I said while rolling my neck at him.

"You right, I don't know her but-,"

Cutting him off, I retorted, "There's no but, Edo. You don't know her, simple, end of fucking discussion." Letting the tears fall down my face in frustration, I ran in the room, slamming the door shut.

Hearing the light taps on the door, "Wifey, c'mon let me in; let's talk about this," he pleaded.

"Edo, just leave me alone. You haven't been around in a few days anyway, so go back to where you were!" I said out of jealousy.

I heard him chuckle, "Is that why you're upset bae? C'mon, you know I got shit to handle." His tapping on the door was annoying the fuck outta me.

I heard Kristen in the distance. "What you did now lover boy?" she asked.

"Talk to her. I'm trying to understand, but she shut me out. I gotta run out and handle some shit," he said, "but when I come back, I'm going to take her out."

Rolling my eyes at his persistence, I shouted from the other side of the door, "I'm not going anywhere with your hoe ass!"

He laughed and shook his head. "I knew you was going to start acting up, but I got something for that juicy ass when I get back."

Hearing his feet move away from the door, I waited a few minutes before I exited the room.

"Girl, what is wrong with you?"

I turned my nose up at her. "Nothing, I'm tired of being locked up in this fucking house. I can't wait until Monday, so I can go back to work," I protested, throwing my hands in the air.

"Kori, it's safer if you stay here. Stop rushing it and enjoy your days off from work."

"Kristen, it's Wednesday, I been locked away since Saturday!" I shrieked. "People don't just stay in no damn house for this long." Grabbing a shot glass and the Patron, I drank two shots.

"Okay, I get it, that's why Edo said he was taking you out tonight," she suggested.

"Girl bye," I said, taking another shot. "I'm going back to my room." I waved her off.

"You just sprung on the dick and mad he have to dip every once in a while," Kristen teased.

"Fuck you!" I spat, walking back to my room. Grabbing my cell phone, I texted Ari.

Kori: hey we have to talk

Ari: baby girl are you okay

Kori: oh now you care if I'm okay, can you just meet

me at this address tomorrow?

Ari: yeah baby girl I can

Dozing off, I looked over and Edo was staring at me. "What are you doing here?"

Edo motioned for me to go to the bathroom. "Get in the shower Kori." I rolled my eyes at his antics. "I'm all yours, just me and you tonight," he tried to convince me.

"Whatever Eladio." Getting in the shower, Edo sat on the toilet watching me intently. Hating that he had me under his spell, I stepped out the shower. No longer able to be mad at him, I told him to join me in the bed.

"You wanna stay in or go out?" he asked.

"I want to stay in and fuck you until my kitty is sore."

Watching him jump up from the bed laughing, he said, "I'ma bring a bottle in here. What's your preference, light or dark?"

I was thinking "dark." I knew I fucked up a few hours ago., I had light liquor but it was something about Henny that made me feel invincible. Edo grabbed my foot, massaging it.

"Tssk." I threw my head back. "Don't you start," I warned him. Glaring in my direction, he pulled my foot into his lap and began to deeply massage my foot. *Shit*, I thought to myself. Not wanting to open my eyes, I felt the glare from Edo.

"You relaxed enough?" he asked.

Displaying a goofy grin, I responded, "Yeah, thanks." Pulling back, I got up to pour me a glass of henny and cranberry juice.

"Come here!" he said.

Edo propped himself up by his elbows, admiring my shape. "You are so sexy girl," he said, licking his lips.

Once I was undressed in nothing but my underwear, I straddled him. Leaning in to kiss his lips, I pushed him back. Grinding against his manhood, he gripped my waist. Lifting me up and placing me on the bed, Edo pulled his shirt over his head while my eyes roamed his chiseled chest. Pulling my boy shorts off, I cocked my legs open, exposing my kitty while Edo stood undressing. I massaged my kitty with my right hand.

"Hurry up, I wanna feel you!" I moaned, biting my bottom lip.

"Shit girl." Edo stepped out of his jeans and grabbed the condom from his pocket.

Once I saw his dick was exposed, I was contemplating if I wanted to go through with this again. He jerked his dick while I masturbated in front of him. "Umm hmm, you ready for this dick?"

Nodding yes, I laid back once he was positioned in between my legs. He lifted me up under him and pulled me down on his dick.

"Tssk, fuck Edo!" I moaned out in ecstasy as he continued to fuck me. "Umm." Biting down on his shoulder blade, Edo turned me over so I could ride him. Now in full control, I bounced up and down on his dick while my hands were up against his chest. Slowly gliding up and down his dick, my kitty juices coated his manhood. Edo grabbed a hold of my breast and gently squeezed my nipple, causing me to become wet all over again.

"Ahhh fuck Edo, I'ma cum!" I shouted.

"Cum on this dick then," he ordered.

Throwing my head back, I sped up the pace as I felt my orgasm nearing. As my kitty pulsated against his manhood, I screamed out in pleasure as I came. "Damé mas papi!" I begged. Edo smirked after I released all over him.

Placing me on the bed, he opened my legs. Licking his way from my neck to my breast, Edo took my left nipple in his mouth and massaged the right one until my nipples were erect. Trailing his spit to my right nipple, he flicked his tongue over it and gently bit down on it. As he kissed his way to my kitty, he planted kisses on my thighs before he kissed my love box. Staring into my eyes, Edo parted my lips and licked my kitty. Sliding his finger inside of me, he continued to use his tongue to lick and suck on my clitoris. Pulling back a little, he blew on my kitty while he finger fucked me.

What the fuck is this man doing to me? I thought as I was reaching yet another climax. Closing my leg on his head, I didn't want to cum just yet. Pulling back from him, I got up. Removing the condom and getting on my knees, I stroked his dick to attention and placed my lips on it. Licking up and down his dick like I saw in the porn, I jerked it while I sucked on his balls. Hearing him moan and grab my bun was all the motivation I needed. Edo was about 9 inches long and I planned to deep throat or at least try. While he held onto my hair, I opened my mouth and sucked on his dick.

"Fuck girl, just like that!"

Relaxing my jaw, I let him face fuck me until I felt the warm precum in my mouth. Slowly releasing his dick, I sucked on the tip until he stopped me. Lifting me up, he turned me around as I positioned myself doggystyle. Throwing it back, he slapped me on my ass while I backed up on his dick. "Cum for me, papi!" Holding onto my hips as he thrust himself in and out of me, I came all on his dick.

"That's that shit!" Making my pussy grip the dick, he moaned as he sped up the pace and his dick pulsated. "Fuck I'm coming!" he shouted while I threw it back. Feeling the warm semen shoot up in me, he held me in place.

Oh, my God, I thought. Collapsing on the bed, I rolled over to my side, catching my breath.

Chapter 13

Ari

I was happy as hell to hear from my girl. I missed her and was happy she decided to give me a chance to explain myself. Looking over at my phone alerting me another text was coming through, I jumped seeing Kori's name.

Kori: Ari I'm not going to be able to meet up with you

Ari: what the fuck you mean Kori?

Kori: listen give me some space I'll link when I'm ready

I didn't even bother responding. I started calling her but to no avail; she kept sending my ass to voicemail until she ended up blocking me. "Fuck." I couldn't understand for the life of me how she just flipped and changed the plans. If I find out she shacking up with someone else, she gon wish the bullet had grazed her ass. Taking out the contents from the baggie, I placed a line on the table and snorted as much as I could.

"Shit." Holding my head back and dabbing my nose, I felt the effect of my high. Relaxing for a few minutes, I jumped up after I thought I heard a sound. "Fuck?" Picking up my house phone, I called Kori repeatedly until she finally answered in a groggily tone. "Bitch, if you don't meet me tomorrow, I'm going to kill you when I get my hands on your hoe ass!"

Hearing shuffling in the back, "Hello, what is the problem?" she said, just above a whisper.

"Koriann, where the fuck are you? I'm tired of playing hide and seek with your ass!"

Clearing her throat, she said, "Calm down okay, it's not that serious-,"

She was cut off by a guy. "I know you not talking to that crazy bitch!" I heard him say and then the phone line went dead.

Vexed, I ran out my apartment and straight to my car. Driving on the Cross Bronx expressway, I noticed a car tailgating behind me. "Shit." Turning off before my exit, the car made the same turn. "Okay, calm down Ari," I chastised.

Adrenaline pumping and my high in full effect had me paranoid. Turning on the block of Kori's grandmother's house, I hopped out the car, heading straight to her basement entrance. I remember Kori once telling me there was a spare key under the mat. Finding the key and fidgeting with the lock, I finally let myself in. Knocking over a table, her grandmother must of heard the movements from upstairs. Climbing the stairs as quietly as I could, the door swung open just as I was reaching for the handle. Scaring her, she grabbed her chest while bending over.

"Fuck!" Panicking, I saw someone knocking on the door. Looking towards the front door, I ran back down the stairs. Checking around the corner, I saw the car was nowhere in sight, so I jogged up the block to my car and left.

Stepping on the gas, I heard sirens from what seemed like an ambulance and decided to get lost. "I hope nothing happened to her." Beating on the steering wheel, I tried calling Kori again. Realizing she wasn't going to answer, I gave up and headed straight to Raj's house.

Chapter 14

Edo

"So, you been talking to that bitch who not only shot you but been beating on you, Kori? I took you for a woman who's smarter than that!" I spewed. Looking at Kori sit in the corner crying, I felt bad for yelling at her but she was playing a dangerous game and, if it came down to someone running up in my house, I would kill them over her silly ass.

"I'm sorry," she spoke almost above a whisper. "I wasn't keeping in contact with her this whole time Edo!" she cried.

I heard banging on the door. "Don't be yelling at my sister, nigga! What y'all not gon keep doing is playing her for no weak bitch!" Kristen shouted. "Kori, let's go!" she ordered her. Kori jumped up from the floor, grabbing her clothes.

"You're not going anywhere Kori, so just have a seat." Opening up the bedroom door, "Kristen look, I understand you're mad at me, but y'all can't go. Matter fact, you can go, but I'm not letting Kori leave and then something happens to her," I stressed, trying to reason.

"Nah, fuck that, you not gon be bossing her around." Looking over at Kori, she stood in the door fully dressed with pleading eyes. Diesel came flying up the stairs.

"Yo Edo, you ain't answering your damn phone and Ty been blowing you up!" He was out of breath.

"Oh shit."

I dialed his number back. "Yo Edo, I been calling you got the past 15 minutes man. Ol girl grandmother had a heart attack and she ain't make it."

"What the fuck? How the hell that happened?" I asked, getting upset.

"Nigga, I don't know. I just know I heard noises and, when I broke down her door, she was passed out." Hearing Chris' voice crack had me fucked up cuz he wasn't no small dude who broke easily.

"Aight man, where y'all at?" Taking down the information, I hung up, turning to Kori and Kristen.

I paced back and forth, not knowing how to tell them. "Kristen and Kori, that was Ty." I paused to study their facial expressions.

"Ok, so what?!" Kristen asked with much attitude.

"Your grandmother suffered a heart attack and didn't make it." Had I not known any better, I would have thought Kori had fainted, the way she fell to the floor. Rushing over to her, Kristen cried in Diesel's arms. "Kori ma, c'mon." I tried picking her up, but she was giving me a fight.

"Why does everybody leave me?" she cried hysterically. Defeated, I let her cry until she could no longer cry. Kristen had eventually retrieved to her room. "Where is my grandma at?" she asked, looking down in disgust.

"At Montifore Hospital." Grabbing up Kori off the floor, Kristen wasted no time.

"Had your crazy bitch not been stalking you, abuela would be fine!"

Looking over at Kristen, I said, "Don't blame her, she doesn't need this right now. Diesel, take her to the car."

"Nah, fuck that, she's the reason mami left and now abuela is gone!" she spat.

Kori looked helpless. "That's not fair Kristen," Kori's voice cracked and she ran down the stairs.

Running after her, "Kori, c'mon, she's mad and needs to blame someone," I tried calming her down. Watching Diesel and Kristen get in his car and pull off, Kori looked lost.

"So now she hates me," she said solemnly, hopping into the passenger seat.

After hours in the hospital, the paperwork was processed to get a move on their grandmother's arrangements. Kristen set it up so she'd be cremated and, being all their family was back in Puerto Rico, she set it up to do it right away.

"I can't believe this," Kori said to no one in particular.

"I'm ready to go back to the house."

Chapter 15

Paris

Calling Edo back to back showed me that he was back on his bullshit. Once I tried for the 15th time, I decided to call my side boo over.

"Hey beautiful wassup?"

"Hey boo, you trying to come over and give me some of that dick?" I asked, getting straight to the point. Edo had been neglecting my sexual needs and I was hot and bothered.

"How about you meet me at my house? I'm not trying to drive out there and I got something special for you," he stressed.

"Ok, say no more, give me about an hour." Ending the call, I scrolled to Edo's name and blocked his number. I'd be damned if I allowed him to miss my dick appointment because he wanted to call and reconcile.

Call me what you want but, when my sexual needs weren't being met, I had to satisfy them. Raj was someone I fucked with from time to time when Edo was acting up. The dick was amazing but he was a pig, so I couldn't fuck with him on any other level or Edo would indeed snap my neck. Pulling up to Raj's house, I noticed another car in his driveway. Raising my brow, I was hesitant about knocking.

"So, you just gon stand out there?" he asked, pulling me in. Walking in, I noticed a chick lying across his couch in nothing but a bra and panties. "Surprise," he said.

Unsure of what games he was playing, I said, "Excuse me?!"

"I told you I had a surprise for you, so I'm bringing my homegirl into our session."

Cocking my head to the side, I said, "Huh?"

The chick got up with glassy eyes and pushed me up against the wall with a great amount of strength. "I want you and he wants you, so what's it gonna be?" she asked.

"Umm shit, ok, you ain't gotta be manhandling me. I've had a threesome before," I said, pushing her up off me. "What's ya name?" I asked her out of curiosity

"Ari."

Chapter 16

Kori

Back at Edo's house, he situated me and said he had to make a run. "How are you going to leave me tonight? I need you," I pleaded.

"Baby girl, I'ma be back. I gotta check on something," he said. "Go ahead and lay down, I'll bring in some food."

Rolling my eyes, I stomped off to the room. Hearing the door close, I grabbed my phone to text Jada. After 5 minutes of no response, I started packing my things. I was not staying here another damn night alone. Noticing that the boys who watched the door wasn't there, I ordered an Uber and left out.

Once I got to the hotel, I called Ari, hoping she would meet me here.

"Hey ma?"

"Ari, meet me please, I need you." I caught myself choking up.

"I'm on my way."

Waiting in the lobby of the hotel for Ari to show up, I thought about what Kristen said about my mother and grandmother. "Hey beautiful." Ari walked up on me.

"I didn't check in yet." Ari went to check in and led me to the room. "She's gone Ari, my abuela died." The tears fell as soon as I said it.

Pulling me into an embrace, Ari said, "Baby, I'm so sorry, come take a bath."

After soaking in the tub for almost an hour, Ari called out to me. Stepping out of the tub, I looked over my face and saw the day's events evident. Sighing heavily, I exited the bathroom wrapped in the robe. "Come here ma, let me make you feel good," Ari said.

"I'm fine. I just want to sleep Ari. Can you just let me sleep?" I asked her.

"If you let me hold you," she retorted.

"Sure." She stripped out of the bathrobe and under the covers in the nude.

Ari headed to the bathroom to shower. I didn't know if the water had burned her, but she screamed out, "That shit burned!" Then, I drifted off to sleep.

I awoke to Ari prying my legs open and her hand rubbing across my kitty. Not wanting to get aroused, Ari knew exactly how to handle me. "Ari stop," I moaned.

"Let me take care of you, Kori."

Looking over at her glassy eyes, I figured Ari had a drink. Falling back onto the bed, I spread my legs, slightly inviting her in. "You been giving my pussy away?" Ari asked, aggressively biting down on my thigh.

"Ouch Ari, that doesn't turn me on the fuck." I tried pushing her off of me.

"Stay still Kori," she warned. Closing my eyes, I figured if I faked an orgasm, she would leave me alone. Ari brought her mouth to my pussy and starting licking and sucking on my clit. Inserting 2 of her fingers as she usually did, she looked up. "Why your pussy not as tight as it was Kori?"

Looking down at her like she was crazy, I asked, "Are you kidding me?"

"I asked you a damn question Kori, now answer me," she spat, gripping my thighs and pulling me down. "You like taking dick?" Ari slapped me across my face.

Fighting back, I began kicking and swinging my arms, knocking Ari off of me. Jumping up, I grabbed the nearest thing to me and flung it at her. Missing her seemed to upset her more and she charged at me full speed, making me fall off the bed. Ari grabbed my neck with her two hands and placed her legs on my arms while I was kicking and clawing at her arms, trying to get her off of me. It must have work because she let me neck go. Watching her breathe heavily, I tried backing away from her and she grabbed my feet, pulling me across the rug.

"Ahhh Ari, that burns!" I cried out, but it fell on deaf ears as she started attacking me. Trying to cover my naked body Ari removed her belt and hit me with it. Balling up while trying to shield my face, she whipped me until my back started to feel numb. With no more tears left in me, something must have caught Ari's attention because she stopped hitting me and stumbled towards her bag.

Picking up her phone, I couldn't hear the caller but I knew it must of been urgent because she hung up quickly, looking for her belongings. "You better not go nowhere Kori, I'll be back." Coming to my side, she tried to touch my face but I jumped. "I'm sorry, I don't know what came over me, but I'm sorry." Not trying to look in her face, I closed my eyes.

The ones you love the most prove to be the ones who hurt you the worst.

Chapter 17

Edo

After running to Paris' house and not seeing her car in the driveway, I began to panic. "Shit," I cursed myself for not coming here sooner. Running to the door, I opened it and the house was dark. After checking every room, I realized Paris had to be gone for a while. Dialing her number back to back, there was no answer. Leaving her a text to get back to me, I waited at the house. Calling Kori, she didn't answer as well; in fact, she sent my ass straight to voicemail. Here I was chasing this old hoe when I should have been laid up with Kori. Leaving out, my work phone started ringing. "Yo Unc, wassup?"

"Listen, I wasn't going to involve you in this shit, but I need you to know that I got a dirty cop who owes me some bread and she ain't pay up yet."

Caught off guard, I questioned, "What, a cop? Unc, are you crazy?!" I had to ask cuz he knew what type of business we were running.

"I ain't got time for the lecturing bullshit. This shit is serious cuz now she owe me double, and I need you to pay Issac a visit. He's the dumb ass that gave her the re-up, but I'ma let her think she good and go after someone that's precious to her!" he roared.

Shaking my head, "Aight Unc, I'll handle it, but what's ol girl name?" I asked outta curiosity.

"Ari." Stunned after he hung up, I put two and two together. "Ain't this about a bitch." Figuring out the someone special may be Kori, I hoped that wasn't her Ari but, then again, she had a gun and the way she had Kori scared told me that definitely was the same Ari.

Calling up Diesel, I broke it down to him as I approached my house. "Yo, that's wild. I'm about to tell Kristen, so she can reach out to her sister."

"Aight, bet. I'm about to see how she feeling since I went running out after Paris," I confessed.

"Nigga, you left her in the house alone? You better hope she ain't get tired of your shit and bounced," he chuckled.

Unlocking the door, the house was seemingly quiet. Racing up the stairs, I looked in the bedroom and noticed clothes thrown around in the room. "Kori!" I shouted, knowing she was gone; I could kick myself for leaving her. "Fuck!"

Calling Kori repeatedly, I prayed she would answer. "Wifey, I know I shouldn't of left, but please call me back." Here I was pussy whipped, calling Kori like she was mine. "Think Edo, where would she go?" I mumbled.

"Yo!"

"Ayo Diesel, where Kristen at? Tell her get ahold of Jada and see if she heard from Kori!" I barked.

"Aight."

Hearing him ask Kristen, it sounded like she started panicking. "She tried to call me." Hearing her cry in the background, I became frustrated.

"Yo, nobody heard from her. Kristen said they both missed her calls."

Sighing, I replied, "Aight bet." Ending the call, I called Dice, my private investigator, to help me locate Kori.

Chapter 18

Deuce

Hearing the stress in Edo's voice, I knew something was bothering him. I only gave him the task of taking care of Issac cuz I wanted to handle Ari my way, and that was going to get her chick she so called loved so much.

"Baby, when are you coming home? You said one night and it's been two!" Marie said into the phone.

"I know ma but, until this is handled, I can't come home; can you understand that?"

She sighed. "Malcolm, you said that you was getting out of the fucking game. Here you are getting trapped right back in this shit!" she spat angrily

"Marie, relax-,"

Cutting me off, "No, if you continue to chase the streets, I will leave and I mean that Malcolm!" she said sternly, hanging up. The only time Marie called me by my government name was when she meant business.

"Yo uncle, wassup?"

"I'm in the city, come link up with me!" I said, pressing the issue.

"Aight, say no more."

I knew Edo's mind was elsewhere but Diesel seemed alert, so I hit him up to see if he could find this bitch and handle what needed to be handled. Pulling up to the restaurant of my choice, I waited for Diesel to arrive. Ordering a double shot, I needed this for the courage to ask him for help in assisting me with Ari.

"Yo Unc, wassup, this meeting just for you and me?" he quizzed.

"Yea, Edo obviously handling some shit, so I wanted to come directly to you and ask you for some extra hands in catching somebody who has gone ghost on a nigga."

He looked over at my empty shot glasses and placed an order. After taking the 2 shots, he looked in direction. "Yo, what we taking about, cuz I've never known you to not have Edo on board."

Chuckling, I knew he was hesitant. After telling him I needed that bitch Ari brought to me in one piece, he seemed to be on board. "Aight, I got you, Unc."

Vibing with Diesel for a bit, I headed back to my hotel, ready to call my wife, jerk my dick to her video, and fall asleep. Edo would hear from me about this Issac situation.

Chapter 19

Ari

Finding out that Deuce wanted my head, I had to think fast and staying in the hotel room under my name was no good. I knew he wasn't going to do shit to Kori, so I bounced. Thinking on my feet, I called my captain. "Ari, you must be caught up in some shit if you're calling me on your vacation," he chuckled like shit was funny.

"Listen captain, my life is in danger and I need a hotel but I can't put it in my name," I stressed.

"What kind of shit you done got yourself into Ari? Listen, when your father disappeared, I said I'd watch after you, but you seem to be always in some shit!" he barked.

"I know, but I promise you it's not my fault this time," I pleaded, trying to convince him. "So you say, come to my house and then you can explain to me what is going on," he lectured.

Trying to call Kori, hoping that I didn't hurt her too bad, she didn't answer my call, sending my thoughts in a frenzy. "Hey captain," I greeted him after entering his house.

"Ari, cut the bullshit; what the hell is going on?"

"Okay, so you won't judge me right?" He gave me a side eye.

"Did I judge your crazy ass when you claimed you was bisexual, or the time you needed to have the abortion or how about-"

Cutting him off with a wave of my hand, I said, "Okay, I get it. No, you haven't anyway. I fucked up. I been snorting coke."

Waiting on his response, his eyes damn near bulged outta his socket. "Yea, I know and, before you say something, I don't know why I started. It was at a party." Pacing the floor, I said, "I'm not addicted yet, but I need to stop."

"You think Ari? Or do you want too?" he asked.

After telling him about the drug using to the beating I just gave Kori, he was disgusted in me. "That still doesn't explain why somebody wants you, Ari."

Thinking quick on my feet, I responded, "Because I beat Kori, so her father is looking for me. He said I'ma dead woman and he's the one who I been buying the coke from," trying to sound as convincing while lying.

"Aight, let's go get you situated, lay low and, when you come back to work, we'll figure out this situation," he assured.

Leaving out with some relief, he booked me a room for a month until everything was situated. I tried calling Kori again, but she had yet to answer me. I know, call me crazy. I beat her ass, then miss her and apologize. I asked captain Jones to go to her room and check on her and make sure she didn't need any medical attention. If she did, this situation could go from bad to worst and I didn't need that type of heat on me.

A couple of months ago, I ran into Deuce at a party and asked to buy some coke from him to make some extra money. After repeatedly being suspended from work, my hours started to become slim to none and I had bills and Kori, who I loved to spoil. The minute she took notice to me being over more, she started questioning my job. I remember the conversation.

"Bae, is everything okay, you been here more often. Did you lose your job?"

Turning around to face her, I answered, "Girl no." I chuckled to hide my nervousness. "I just haven't had to be in the field much."

She simply replied, "Okay," and left it alone. So, when opportunity presented itself and Deuce could have an officer on his payroll, he was willing to work with me.

After a few weeks of doing exactly what I told him, he started giving me more work. One day I was stressed because I had indeed got suspended after fighting one of the other female officers, I went home panicking. Unlike my other suspensions, this one was on the books and I feared losing my job.

Sitting at home, I needed to take the edge off, so I snorted some coke. The high I felt as my adrenaline rushed had me instantly hooked. That night, I went to Kori's house and we had a physical fight, resulting in her having a busted lip and bruised leg. I should have stopped using that day but, the more I dug myself deeper, the more I started using and the more I took my anger out on Kori.

Chapter 20

Kori

Finding the strength to pull myself off of the floor, my body ached tremendously, but I knew I had to get out of this room before Ari showed her face again. I didn't know what came over her but, for the past few months, she had been kicking my ass and it had gotten worst every time. Locating my phone, I contemplated who to call. Turning my phone on, there were tons of messages. I knew if I returned Kristen or Jada's call, they would want to hunt Ari down, so I settled on calling Edo.

"Baby, where are you?"

At the mere sound of his voice, I broke down, telling him everything that happened. "I'm bringing you a sweat suit to put on; try to fix yourself up ma." He assured me he would be at the hotel in less than 10 minutes. Relieved, I brushed my hair and put as much makeup on my face to cover the bruising that started to show. I begged him not to tell Kristen just yet; there had to be a plan and I really didn't want her getting in trouble with the law.

Looking over my reflection in the mirror, I was pissed. Never in my life had I ever been referred to as no punk bitch, but it seemed like Ari had some damn super strength that overpowered me.

Hearing the knock on the door, I made sure not to make a sound. I knew the visitor couldn't be Edo because he promised he would text when he was on his way up. After what felt like a few minutes, the person stopped knocking and must have left, since I heard the elevator bell. Sighing, I hoped that wasn't Ari so, out of panic, I texted Edo.

Kori: please hurry I'm scared

Edo: I'm coming upstairs now

Kori: k

Rushing to the door, I heard the bell again. Pulling open the door, Edo slipped in, looking over my appearance. Embarrassed, I hung my head low in shame. Lifting my chin with his hand, he said, "Baby, you don't have to be ashamed, I'm here now." Pulling me in for an embrace, I cried on his chest. "C'mon ma, let me get you outta here."

Helping me get dressed, he grabbed my bags. Pulling out my Chanel oversized sunglasses and putting them on, we exited the room and hotel. Easing into the seat, my back stung sliding back in the chair.

"Why didn't you call me sooner?" he asked, concerned.

"Because you had played me, Eladio. You left when I needed you the most." I strained my voice cuz it was hoarse after Ari damn near choked the life out of me.

"And I'm sorry for that Kori, do you trust me?" he asked.

"Yea," I sighed, blocking everything out as Edo drove to the house.

Pulling up to the house, Edo stopped me. "You know I have to take care of this, right."

Rolling my eyes, I stressed to him that it was a bad idea to retaliate. "Edo, just leave it alone, please. She's a cop and it won't end well Edo."

After days of healing in the house, I was ready to return back to work. I was confident that Ari wouldn't show up there and mess with me, besides the fact I hadn't heard from her anyway.

"You sure about going to work? I think you should let your body heal a little more," he suggested, running his hand down my back. The marks on my back and arms were still visible, so I settled on a black, long sleeve BeBe dress and pumps.

"Yea bae, I'm fine to go to work and I don't want to be in this house locked away like last time," I whined.

Throwing his hands up in defeat, he said, "You got it, but I'm dropping you off and picking you up."

After thinking about it, I replied, "Guess I'll have to just deal with that." I smiled at how overprotective Edo was.

"You know you wifey, so I don't know why you think I'ma let you put yourself in harm's way again"

"I know, I know." Pecking him on his lips, I grabbed up my Louis Vuitton bandouliere purse and headed to the car.

"Keep switching that ass like that, you won't be going into work," he warned.

"Umm hmm, I'll give you this pussy and it's gon knock your ass out," I said while laughing, "and I'll still go to work," I challenged.

"Yea aight, you know I'll tear that little pussy up; have that shit sore." Walking up on me, he grabbed my ass. I pushed his hand away because we didn't have time to play any games.

"Baby stop, c'mon, just take me to work," I whined.

"Bet, just be ready to bust that shit open tonight." He smiled, showing his pearly white teeth.

Life was getting back on track. Ari seemed to disappear and, the day I decided to stop by my apartment to see if everything was in order, I found it: the little baggy in the nightstand draw on Ari's side as I called it. With wide eyes, everything started to make sense. The change in her behavior, the careless mistakes she started making, the rage she felt and would attack me for no reason. *Ain't this about a bitch*, I thought. *This damn chick a drug addict.* Sitting on my bed, I tried to think about when she started acting out, how long had she been using, and if her ass was getting help.

Leaving out of the condo obviously upset, something hit me and everything went black.

Chapter 21

Paris

After meeting Ari at Raj's house, I wanted to keep engaging in them threesomes with her, but she disappeared and it went back to just casual sex with Raj. Edo decided he wanted to start missing in action again and I prayed for the moment I got back in touch with him. Calling up my homegirl Daisha, I needed a night out. Deciding on having dinner instead of our usual club scene, she opted to bring one of her cousins along to our outing. Rolling my eyes as I entered the restaurant, I spotted Daisha and made my way over to her. Looking her cousin over, I noticed she was a pretty girl, with natural curls and cocoa complexion. She smiled, displaying 2 deep dimples.

"Hello," she greeted.

Shooting her a smile, I said, "Hey."

Turning to Daisha, she said, "Hey girl." After catching up with each other and our orders were placed, Daisha wasted no time spilling tea.

"Girl, I didn't know you and Edo had split up," she said, popping her tongue.

Turning up my nose and rolling my eyes, "Who told you that?" I inquired.

"Girl, nobody had to tell me. I saw him at the mall with some other chick, and they were boo'd up girl."

I rolled my eyes. "Stop lying, always starting shit," the girl at the table spoke up.

"Yea, he's dating my homegirl, and he never mentioned you," she stated matter of factly.

I held everything in me from going across the table and knocking this bitch upside her head. "Who is your friend?" I questioned her, staring directly in her eyes.

"I'm not about to give you my girl name and you go looking for her. Hell no."

Folding her arms, I reached across the table trying to snatch this bitch up, but Daisha caught me before my hand landed on her. "Bitch, you must not know about me!" I shouted.

"I don't care who you are, go check your so called man. How about don't even do that cuz my friend got him hooked on her tight pussy!" she laughed.

"Daisha, let me get outta here. I don't be doing this ghetto shit your homegirl on." She waved at Daisha. "I'm going to call you later cousin."

After her cousin left, I spazzed out. "Listen, I only didn't commence to whooping her ass cuz she's your cousin, but ol girl better not cross me when you're not around!"

"Do what you please but, trust, my cousin ain't no punk and what she said was right. I'm sure your ass ain't gonna give up your homegirl name to a chick she don't know." Shrugging, Daisha got up. "You might want to check Edo yourself."

"If you had brought that up to just me instead of broadcasting that shit, I would of handled it differently," I stated while flaring my nose, "but I'm out." Leaving the restaurant, I headed straight to where I know Edo would have no choice to be at.

Pulling up to one of the stash spots, I noticed Diesel's car out front. "Bingo." If Diesel was here, then more than likely Edo wasn't far behind him. Banging on the front door causing a scene, Diesel came flying out.

"Yo, what the fuck Paris? You trying to make this shit hot?" he asked.

Staring at him blankly, "Where is Edo and, before you lie, think about me causing a real scene Diesel?!" I said through gritted teeth.

"Stay your ass right here," he warned.

I heard him telling Edo to get his ass over here now and how I was a crazy bitch. I could care less, as long as Edo brought his ass here ASAP. Watching his black Range Rover pull up to the block and him leaving it on, he headed straight in my direction.

"What the fuck wrong with you, yo?" he asked, grabbing on my arm and pulling me towards his car.

Pulling my arm back, I slapped him across his face. "So, you out here doing you, huh?!" Edo never put his hands on me before but, after seeing his reaction, I jumped back cuz I knew I had it coming.

"Get the fuck in the car!" he challenged.

Taking heed to his threats, I hopped in the car. "How could you stop fucking with me? Who's this new bitch?" I screamed, letting my emotions get the best of me.

Edo looked over at me. "You could have brought unnecessary attention to us, cuz you're acting like a jealous bitch!"

Snapping my neck, "A jealous bitch?" I questioned, putting my fingers in his face. "First of all, we are a couple, so how can I be jealous when you are mine!"

"Yours? Paris, I ain't no damn property. You see this is exactly why this shit ain't gon work. You don't know when to relax; you too old for the shit and, while you out here showing your ass, where Parnell?"

Looking at me with daring eyes, I responded, "He's with his grandmother."

"Exactly." Before I could respond to his smart remark, his phone started ringing. Looking at the middle console, I saw a pic flash across the screen displaying the word 'wifey'.

"Oh, hell no." Thinking quick, I grabbed it.

"Put my phone down yo."

"Nah, I'ma answer this shit," I threatened. Looking at the chick, I knew this had to be the bitch Jada was referring too. "Hello?"

"Who is this?" the caller asked, sounding more like a male than a female. Playing along so Edo wouldn't notice, "Oh, you don't know about me. This is Edo's girl and have been for the past few years!" I shouted and the phone line went dead. Fighting with Edo to keep the phone away from him while he drove, I was lying it on thick so he would believe that I was still on the phone. "Yea, and we have a family so leave him the fuck alone!"

Acting as if I hung up, I said, "So, this is the shit you do? I'm pregnant!" I shocked myself saying that cuz I was indeed not, but I needed to think fast so that he would come back to me.

Edo swerved the car so hard, almost hitting a parked car. "By who?" he asked.

"What you mean? I only been fucking you?"

He gave me a side eye. "Bitch, I strap up every fucking time and you claim to be on birth control miss. I don't want anymore kids!"

Pulling up in front of a Duane Reade "What are we doing here?" I quizzed.

"Oh, you're going to take a test and, if you are pregnant, then we discuss what is next" He mugged me while pushing me in the store.

Arriving at the house, I tried to stall with taking all three of the tests Edo brought. "Get in that bathroom Paris and take the damn test. I ain't got time for this bullshit!"

"No, you just wanna make sure that whoever wifey is is good," I said, quoting with my hands. I didn't tell Edo that I wasn't talking to no female on the other line because he surely would have left; maybe it was her man and he found out about her and Edo fucking around.

Grabbing the test, I went to the bathroom; Edo followed right behind me. "Where are you going?"

"Bitch, I done saw ya pussy before, so this ain't no different; pee on them sticks!" Opening the packaging, I peed on all three. Passing it to Edo, the look on his face was of shock. "Your ass really trying to trap a nigga huh? How the fuck you end up pregnant? You been fucking with the condoms Paris!" he shouted, knocking them off the sink.

Stunned by what he said, I said, "No, I haven't, maybe it broke," trying to reassure him.

Edo came up ready to choke the life out of me. "I gotta get outta here yo." Edo left out the house, slamming the door. I was thinking what the fuck did I just get myself into? How the hell was I pregnant, and Edo was right; I didn't want another child. Shit, I didn't want Parnell, but his daddy promised me the world, that was until they locked his simple ass up. Shaking my head, I had to make an appointment and fast; there may still be hope for an abortion.

Chapter 22

Edo

After leaving Paris' crib, I was pissed the hell off. Pulling out my phone calling Kori, the call went straight to voicemail. "I'm tired of this phone game shit," I mumbled. Every time Kori got mad, she would block me, then go leave the house. Racing to my house, I noticed it was how I left it; iron still on the counter, glasses still in the sink and Kori shoes right by the door. All the things Kori would have handled as soon as she got in, especially leaving her red bottoms by the door was not something she would leave after she came in. Thinking fast, I ran to the bedroom, opening the closets and drawers. Nothing was out of place, so she hadn't packed any bags.

So, what the fuck, was all I was thinking. *Where is this girl?* Kori went to work and was usually home by 5; it was damn near 7 and she had yet to step foot in the house. Panic came over me. What if Ari's ass caught up with her? Sighing heavily, I was thinking this was exactly why I told her let me continue taking and picking her up. I called Kristen to see when she heard from her last. "Aye sis, you heard from Kori today?" I asked while trying not to alarm her

"Yea, we were going to meet up after she swung by her old crib to grab something, but then she canceled and said she'd rather be laid up under your ass," she chuckled.

"So, she went by her old apartment right after work?"

"Yea, she called me when she got there. Is something wrong?"

Not wanting to answer yes, I replied, "Oh nah, where Diesel at?" She passed him the phone. "Yo bro, meet me at Kori old spot and don't say shit to Kristen," I warned.

Seeing Kori's car in the complex parking lot, I ran up the stairs with Diesel following close behind me. Noticing the door slightly opened, I pulled out my gun. Entering the apartment, nothing looked out of place, just like at my house. I went from room to room and that's when Diesel called me downstairs.

"Yo, this look like blood Edo." By the door, it looked like blood specs. Examining the spot, it sure did and that's when I noticed her chain off to the side; the one she never took off. It also held some ashes from her grandmother.

Picking it up, it was popped. "Fuck, somebody got her." Pacing back and forth, I said, "If that bitch got her, I'ma kill her!" I raced out of the condo.

"Where you going Edo?"

"I'm paying Issac a visit. It's long overdue and because of his carelessness, that bitch Ari owes Unc money and she could be behind this too."

Running into Issac wasn't hard. I just stalled cuz I knew what had to be done. Spotting him leaving one of the stash houses, I grabbed my gun and walked up on him. "Yo bruh, let me holla at you." On instinct, Issac tried to run, but it was short lived by Diesel stepping in, hitting him with the butt of his gun. "The fuck you think you going?" Issac stumbled.

Grabbing him up, I pulled him into the house. "Yo nigga, you been ducking me for a minute now. You got something to hide?" I asked. I ordered the the young boys to sit him in the chair.

"Yo Edo, man, what the fuck? I ain't did nothing to you yo," he tried, pleading his case.

"Nigga, you fucking with my uncle and fucking with him means fucking with me!" I spat.

"I don't know what you talking about. I would never do no shit to Deuce," he said, holding his hands up. "Listen Edo, we go way back, so tell me what this is about."

I punched him in the face. "Nigga, you fronted that bitch Ari some coke after her ass already was in debt!" Looking around, Issac was stuck. "Yea, you ain't think Mark and them was gon snitch on you, right? Well, surprise bitch." I pulled my nine and pointed it at his chest. "Yo Edo, I got kids man!" he tried pleading.

"Yea, I'll make sure to tell ya bm you cost yourself your life nigga!"

"Yo Edo, c'mon man. I'll tell you where that bitch stay at man," he started stuttering.

"Nigga, that bitch got my wife snatched up all because you fronted her some work; now, she on the run with my girl!" Pulling the trigger before he could respond, I emptied three bullets in his chest. Turning to the young boys, I said, "Clean this shit up and, if one of y'all bring me Ari, I'll look out for y'all."

"Yo, I can't believe Issac did no shit like that. He better be glad you got to him before Deuce," Diesel said, hopping in my car.

"Yea, I know, but now I don't know where the hell Ari got Kori and, until I get her back alive, there was going to be bloodshed."

Chapter 23

Kori

After waking up in a room, I noticed I wasn't restrained or anything. Easing off of the mattress, I looked over and nothing looked familiar. Rubbing the side of my head, I spotted the blood that had dried on my scalp. "Shit." The agonizing pain that shot through my head caused me to fall back into the mattress.

"You're awake?" someone said and the voice was oh so familiar.

"What are you doing to me? Just let me go, Ari. This shit is draining and I'm ready to have my man put a bullet in your stupid ass!" I said, rolling my eyes.

"Your man, huh? You mean that dude Edo?" she quizzed, tapping my phone. "It's funny because I don't know how much longer he's going to be your man, let alone a free man," she chuckled.

Looking at the sinister look in her eyes, I asked, "What are you talking about Ari?"

She sat beside me on the bed. "He's not going to be free much longer, so I don't know how that's going to work out for you." Shrugging her shoulders, she continued, "You're mine until I say you're not!"

Fed up with the back and forth bullshit, "You're a coke head Ari and, the faster you get help, the better it is for your health!" I spat.

Ari started laughing until she was doubling over, grabbing her stomach; apparently, the whole ordeal was funny. "Sweetie, he's not your man. That guy got a baby on the way," she stated matter of factly.

Rolling my eyes, I said, "Give me my phone Ari." She tossed the phone to my side. "I don't know how you know that, but your sources aren't reliable."

Jumping up, she challenged, "Ask him who's Paris and if she's carrying his baby then?"

Not in the mood for any games, I stepped into the bathroom, closing and locking the door. Calling Edo, I waited for his answer. "Baby, where are you? You good?" he asked as soon as the call connected.

"Yea, I'm good. I need to know something Edo?"

"Anything beautiful."

Thinking if I should beat around the bush, I got straight to the point. "Do you have a baby on the way and with a chick named Paris?" The phone line went silent "Hello, Edo, did you hear me?"

Hearing him sigh heavily, he responded, "Listen Kori, this was before me and you-"

Cutting him off, I stated, "Edo, I don't need the excuses, save them. Thanks for keeping me safe, but I'm good."

Ending the call, Edo called me right back. "Ma c'mon, let me see you and talk to you," he pleaded.

"Edo, I'm not even going to sell you dreams. I'm not about to be no stepmother or deal with no baby mama drama, so do me a favor and lose my number." Ending the call this time, I hurried and put him on the block list.

Knocking on the bathroom door pulled me from my thoughts. "Was I lying?" Ignoring Ari's sarcasm, I let the tears fall.

"How the hell was I this naive when it came to Edo," I mumbled to myself. Leaving out the bathroom, Ari jumped to her feet.

"You want me to run you a bath Kori? Fuck that nigga. He was only trying to woo you, so he could get at me. Edo doesn't care about you, girl. Think about it. Every time you needed him, he wasn't there, right?"

Looking in her direction, I rolled my eyes. "Whatever Ari and you're better for me, right?"

"Kori, you may not think it, but I am. I have been using and I'm willing to get help. I just need you to have my back," she pleaded.

"You know I fucked him, right?" Watching her face turn into a scowl, I knew I shouldn't have told her, but it was going to come out one day. "So, you willing to be with me still?"

"Yea Kori," she sighed. "Just make that a thing of the past please."

Chuckling, I thought of the countless orgasms Edo had given me. "Make drug using a thing of the past," I snapped.

Leaving Ari sitting on the bed, I went to the bathroom. "Kristen, don't be worried about me. I'm good and please don't tell Edo where I am," I pleaded.

"Okay, but why not? Don't tell me you're back with that crazy bitch?"

"No, I'm not, just need time."

After talking to for another few minutes, I ended the call. Searching online for rehabs for Ari, I found two matches in PA. "Look at these, you said you didn't want to be close to here so check these two out."

Within a week, I had taken a leave of absence from work with the excuse of caring for a family member and me and Ari headed to Pennsylvania. Not looking back.

Chapter 24

Kristen

Hearing the banging on the front door, I ran after Diesel to see who was causing a ruckus. I heard a female voice shout from the other side, "Desmond, I know you're in there! Diesel!" she shouted, kicking at the door.

Swinging open the door, "The fuck? Rochelle, have you lost your damn mind?!" Diesel spat, pulling her in. "You gon have my neighbors calling the cops on me cuz you wanna be out here acting a fool. Where my son at bitch!" he roared.

Clearing my throat, "Diesel, don't do that," I chastised.

She looked over in my direction. "Who the fuck are you?"

Snapping my neck, I answered, "Listen hoe, don't come up in our spot talking like somebody owe your ass an explanation"

Rolling my eyes, I said "I'll be in the kitchen while you handle this situation Diesel." After walking away, I heard her calling me too many bitches and hoes. "Diesel, you better check her before I beat the brakes off her old ass!" I said over his shoulder.

"Rochelle, unless you bringing Lil Dee, that's the only time you're invited. I'm not going to have you disrespecting my girl," I heard him say. I didn't understand why dudes didn't think about the chicks they fucked until they ended up knocked up. Now, I gotta deal with this ghetto hoe off the strength of Diesel.

Rochelle was the baby mama from hell, unlike his other baby mama Jewel who was less hostile. Rochelle was too damn old to be acting like a kid, and she was money hungry. I kept telling Diesel he needed to try to get custody of Lil Dee.

"She got one more time to play with me and I'm going to knock her the fuck out," he spat.

Although I wasn't for him disrespecting his baby mamas in my face, Rochelle had to learn her place. Not only was she making problems for them but also putting Lil Dee through the ringer with her bipolar and money hungry antics.

"When are you going to take her ass to court? She doesn't need all the money she's getting and she hardly has Lil Dee; he's always here with us," I stressed.

"I'm not going that route. You know the system hates black men. Get dressed, I need to meet up with someone in Cross County. You can pick up some clothes; we need a vacation," he ordered.

Not one to argue with the needing a vacation, I didn't even protest. When we returned, I'd look into him getting custody of Lil Dee, so we could get rid of this bitch. Checking my Facebook, I typed in Kori's name to see if she had any updates and, to my surprise, she had either blocked or deleted her page. I shook my head. "This girl always doing the most." I shot her a text.

Kristen: Sup sis I miss you, hope you good

Waiting for more than 5 minutes for a response, I said a prayer and hoped that she was good and would come around soon. "Diesel, when we come back, can you call your uncle and see if he can help me find my hard headed sister?"

"Yeah, I'll see what I can do. I don't know why she just disappeared and didn't even let Edo explain to her what was going on?"

Shrugging, I didn't have the answers. I just knew at this point, I needed a resolution.

Chapter 25

Edo

Words couldn't describe the anger that went through my body the night Kori dismissed me without me giving an explanation or apology. I knew Ari had something to do with it and, before I allowed her to take my girl and make me look like a bitch, I was going to deliver her to Deuce so he could finish what he started. Paris was clear as day pregnant, but I knew deep down inside that wasn't my seed she was carrying and, until a DNA test proved it, I wasn't claiming shit.

Pulling up to the Jamaican spot on 219th and White Plains Road, Kristen had been texting me for the past few hours, asking about Kori and what happened. "Sis listen, you know your sister is good for running but, if I find out that she's with Ari, I'm going to shake her up a bit cuz she playing with me!" I was not one to give my heart to any chick, that was until I met Kori. I wanted to show her off and cut off all my hoes just to be with her, and she couldn't see that I would kill any and everybody in my way until I got her right in front of me. Diesel and Kristen was headed to Cancun, and I was stuck here pacifying a bitch that was obviously cheating on me.

"Yo Paris, I'm bout to head to you. Get dressed, I got you some breakfast," I spoke into the phone.

Paris insisted I come to this appointment with her, saying it would probably make me happier about the pregnancy if I witnessed the ultrasound firsthand. Me, on the other hand, I had questions and needed to know exactly when she got pregnant.

Walking in the house, it was dirty as always. "I'll be outside." Putting the food on the table, I couldn't stand for a girl to live nasty. Had I seen all these signs before, I would have been cut her off. After fifteen minutes, Paris came out with some lint ball leggings and an oversized tee. Shaking my head in disgust, I unlocked the door.

"Hey baby." She tried reaching over to kiss me.

"Go ahead with that shit Paris." The entire ride was silent, just like I liked it while vibing to A Boogie. Registering in the clinic, I spotted Jada sitting on the opposite side. Trying to avoid her gaze, she got up and headed my way. "Shit," I mumbled.

"So, what was all that shit you was talking before Paris?!" Jada said, walking up on Paris.

Thinking on my feet, I retorted, "Aye Jada, we in a hospital and she's pregnant!" I jumped up, trying to shield Paris from getting hit.

"Nah Edo, she pop a lot of shit. I told her I'd see her sooner than later," Jada said, trying to break free of my grasp. Paris must have felt like I could hold an angry Jada back.

"I said what I said bitch... ain't nobody scared of you-" Before Paris could finish rolling her head, Jada reached over me, popping her in the mouth.

"Keep talking hoe," she said, breaking free of my grasp. "I'm good Edo, I'ma see that hoe as soon as she drop, on my cousin!" she spat, turning to walk away.

"Paris, are you serious? You're pregnant and still acting like a damn bird." I turned to look at her holding her bloody lip. "You better be glad that's all she did," I said while shaking my head. As soon as I was about to get up outta there, the doctor called Paris' name.

Entering the room, I waited while she did her usual checks. When it was time to look at the ultrasound, I asked, "So doctor, can you tell me when she got pregnant?"

The doctor looked at me weird. "Yes, I can." She looked over at Paris, who looked uneasy. "Well, according to the baby's growth and her last period, Paris is 12 weeks pregnant."

Clenching my jaw, I looked over at Paris. "This baby ain't mine and I'm not about to sit through this bullshit. I hope you find the dude who knocked you up though!" Storming out of the room, I headed straight to my car. "I can't believe this bitch tried to get me to be here for her ass."

Starting up the car, I saw a distraught Paris racing towards my car. "How can you not claim our baby Edo? I'm pregnant by you. I haven't cheated on you!"

Dismissing her, I said, "I ain't got time for this shit." I pulled off, heading straight to my uncle's house. These women were driving me crazy and I needed some advice from the woman who raised me: Marie.

Chapter 26

Marie

After receiving the call from Edo, I patiently waited for him to tell me what was stressing him out. I raised Edo since he was 8 years old, after his mom died with his uncle. Setting a plate aside for him and a cup so he could have his usual cup of Henny, I started sipping my wine.

"Auntie, where you at?" he called out.

"I'm back here!" I called out from the kitchen area. Watching him stagger over to me, he went to wash his hands.

"You must of known I could use this good meal right," he chuckled.

"Well, if you having as much girl drama as you say you are, then I'm sure they're not cooking for you," I bragged, passing him the bottle.

"So, where your husband at?" I side eyed him. "Y'all must be beefing if you're referring to him as such." Every time Deuce and Edo would argue, one or the other would refer to each other as a kin to me. It'd been like this ever since Edo became a teen and started speaking out against Deuce.

"So, what chick is stressing you out?" I quizzed, as he ate the last of his rice and beans.

"Paris, she tried to pull the okie doke and said a baby she's pregnant with is mine, knowing damn well I strap up every single time."

I gave him the I told you so face. "Didn't I tell you to stop fucking with her in the first place? She's a hood rat and she will bring you down faster than you think Eladio," I tried to remind him. "I told you to stop dating them hood chicks and find you a real woman with substance and a future that doesn't revolve around your money."

He sat quiet for a minute, taking in everything that I said. "I kinda found a woman, but she ran away when she found out about Paris being pregnant."

I threw up his hands. "So, you're giving up Eladio? I didn't raise you to give up, now did I?" I cleaned up the kitchen while we continued to talk.

"So Eladio, let me ask you something between the both of us," I chastised.

"Okay auntie, shoot."

"Have you been seeing your uncle lately? Something about him seems off and I know when my gut feeling says to follow it, that's what I'm going to do." Edo looked unsure about my questioning.

"I mean, I ain't been seeing him, but I have been keeping in touch; why, wassup?!" Shaking my head, I knew something was off, but I couldn't put my finger on it.

"Nothing. Like I said, I just don't like how he's been moving lately, but do me a favor and get in contact with the young lady who you claim you care about and bring her by so I can meet her. I heard Diesel got him a girlfriend too," I clarified.

"Yea, they're sisters," he boasted.

After Eladio left, I tried calling my husband again but was only sent to his voicemail system. Fearing the worst, I called him lawyer Mr. Andrews, so I could verify that he wasn't locked up. Once I got confirmation that he wasn't locked up, I knew now that Deuce was definitely up to no good and, the minute I put my finger on it, he was going to be mad he fucked with me.

Chapter 27

Kori

Leaving with Ari was probably not the smartest move but, at the rate I was going, I needed a change in scenery. After getting her situated in the outpatient rehabilitation center, I used my free time to check out a spa that was down the block. Lately, I had been feeling sick and lazy, probably due to all the drama I'd endured over the past few weeks, but I knew I needed a recharge. I decided to not keep in touch with anyone because I already knew what was going to come from answering them.

"Why did you leave?", "Where are you going?", "Give him another chance." Those were things I wasn't ready to hear, so muting the world was something I opted to do. Logging into my Facebook account, I saw I had a few unread messages but one in particular caught my eye. It was from Raj, Ari's partner. Not sure what he could want with me, he asked could we meet and said that it was urgent,

Rolling my eyes, I said, "Nope, I'm not responding to him." Closing back out of my Facebook, I sat in the chair getting a deep tissue massage. Once the masseuse started working down my side and back, I felt the urge to vomit. Jumping up from the chair, I grabbed my towel, throwing up all of my breakfast in the trash. Embarrassed and pissed off, I paid the receptionist and hauled my ass to the nearest drug store.

Looking down at the test, my hands stared to sweat and feel clammy. I thought I'd never have to buy one of these being I was with a woman but, after meeting Eladio, he made me realize I indeed loved his dick. Rushing to the apartment, I hurried to the bathroom. Once I peed on both sticks, it showed I was in fact pregnant. Sighing heavily, I knew I had to eventually tell Edo, being that Kristen was dating Diesel.

"Fuck," I mumbled. There was no way I could hide a pregnancy from Ari either. I planned on leaving her once she completed her 30 days in the rehab but, until then, I said I was going to stick by her, just like she had when my grandmother died. Feeling angry and hurt, I called it an early night. I wouldn't have to deal with Ari until the weekend when she got a pass to stay out. Wishing my grandmother was here to talk me through what I should do next, I thought about my mother whom abandoned Kristen and me when we were kids. It was then at that moment that I realized I was definitely alone. With Edo having a baby with another woman, I didn't even know if I could go through with this pregnancy or not, but I was too terrified to even think of an abortion.

Weighing my options, I knew it was wise to just contact Edo, but something in my heart told me I was making the mistake of my life. Dialing his number, I called his phone blocked a few times. After the third call, a female answered his phone; that was enough for me to say fuck it.

Chapter 28

Raj

I had been trying to reach Ari for the past couple of days and she was not answering none of my messages. I had even went as far as to contact Kori, telling her it was an urgent matter. "Raj think, where could this girl be?" A few days ago, some dudes paid a visit to my house looking for Ari, and they told me I better get in contact with them or I was going to end up dead. I wasn't risking my life for her ass cuz she was mixed up in unnecessary drama.

Picking up my ringing phone, I answered, "Yo!"

"Raj, where are you? We need to talk!" I heard Paris say, but I hated hearing that damn phrase.

"About what Paris?"

"Raj, can we just link up please? I really have to talk to you and it can't be over the phone," she stressed. Agreeing to meet her on 149th street and 3rd Avenue by Perry's diner, I arrived a few minutes after her. Paris looked agitated and her eyes were red, as if she was crying.

"Sup girl?"

"Hey," she said in a low tone. "Listen, I don't want to beat around the bush, so I'm pregnant." She dropped the bomb on me.

"Wasn't you fucking with that thug ass nigga?" I asked, trying to see where I fit in on this news.

"It's not his Raj, it's yours," she tried convincing me.

"Check this out Paris. You're not going to pin no baby on me, when there's no way that could be my seed."

Paris looked like I had told her something she didn't know. "Paris, I told you I had a vasectomy years ago so that ain't my seed." Pointing to her stomach, I said, "You better find out who seed you carrying."

Not waiting for her to give me a response, I got up and left. Paris had a lot of nerve telling me I was the father to her unborn seed. Dodging a bullet with her, I headed straight to my house to finish packing up some items for vacation. Turning the corner onto my block, I spotted 2 black cars sitting in front of my building. It was nice outside and Co-Op city was always lined up with cars. Stepping off my elevator, the same two guys who paid me a visit before were at my door waiting for me. "Shit."

"Don't even try to run, Raj. Where is she?" the heavier one asked.

"Listen, if I knew, I would give her up. I told you I haven't seen or heard from her," I stressed.

"I think you lying to us."

"Listen, I could call her right now!" I barked, fed up that they were trying to make me look weak. "What the fuck she mixed up in?" I questioned.

"Don't worry about it. Just make sure the minute you see her, you point us in the direction." The smaller one turned to walk away.

"Uh huh." Turning into my apartment, the larger one hit me with the butt of his gun.

"Don't fuck with us. Your mother would be disappointed if she knew the reason behind her death was her son hiding a conniving bitch."

Watching them step off, I held my head while pulling out my phone to call Ari again. After numerous calls of me not reaching her, I gave up. I paced back and forth thinking what the fuck my next move was going to be?

Chapter 29

Diesel

Vacation was exactly what me and Kristen needed. After Rochelle showed her ass, I had to get her away from Kristen before she beat her ass. Upon arriving home, I dropped Kristen off and went to go meet up with Deuce like he instructed.

"Playa playa, let me holla at you."

"Yo, wassup." I dapped him up.

"I need you to take a trip with me in a couple of weeks. I need you to keep this between me and you, no one can know."

Looking at him strangely, I replied, "Copy, but since when we keeping secrets?"

"You know Edo is a hot head. I can't afford him losing his cool and making me lose a deal that I been working on for a minute."

"Aight, say no more." Not convinced with the meeting that we just had, I knew I had to be leery of what he was getting me mixed up in.

Exiting his office, I called up Edo. "Yo bro, I'm back in the city. We gotta link up cuz Matt said the drop came through," I said on the burner phone.

"Say less, I'ma meet you at the spot" Edo said, hanging up.

Looking over the product that was shipped, I was impressed at how they managed to get everything to us with no problem. "I see they kept their word on their delivery," Edo said, checking it out as well.

"Yea, so should we inform Deuce that the Dominicans are on board?" I quizzed, trying to see what his response would be.

"Yea, let em know and then we could see what our next move will be as far as setting up meetings."

Rubbing my beard, I was trying to piece together why Deuce wanted to conduct meet ups without Edo, if he wasn't doing anything suspicious. Keeping my guards up, I couldn't put Edo on to game, but lying to my bro was something I wasn't happy about.

Chapter 30

Paris

Getting turned down by Edo and Raj, I knew it was only one other person who could be my child's father, but I knew he wouldn't want me to have the baby. He was married and, on more than one occasion, he said he wanted nothing more from me then to just fuck, and I failed by stopping my birth control to get pregnant by Edo. Although I said I didn't want the baby in the beginning, getting pregnant by him had my wheels turning. He was paid, feared and could leave his legacy to my baby. Since his wife never gave him any kids, he had none. I didn't know how I planned to have him accept my baby, but it had to be well thought out because he would kill me if he felt like I was trying to play him.

Then, there was the fact his wife would find out about us and she didn't look like one to be fucked with, even though I'd only heard her on the phone and saw pictures of her.

Calling Ari's phone, it answered on the third ring. "Hey boo, I was just thinking about you!" I cooed into the line.

"Paris?" a girl spoke.

"Yeah, who the hell is this and where is Ari?!"

"Oh, ain't this about a bitch!" the female said into the line. "Aren't you pregnant by Edo, so I'm trying to understand why you calling Ari's phone?"

Chuckling, I knew this had to be her chick. "Oh, she knows why I'm calling her, so you don't worry yourself with it," I laughed and she hung up. I was hot and horny and had no one to please me. I knew calling him would be a waste, but I decided to try my luck anyway.

"You've reach Deuce, leave me a message and I'll holla." Rolling my eyes, I felt the tears well up in my eyes as I fought to hold them back. I was a wreck, an emotional wreck, pregnant yet again by someone who wanted nothing to do with me.

Chapter 31

Kori

Once I hung up on Paris, I was livid. Not only was Edo fucking with her, but now Ari clearly had something going on with her. Picking back up Ari's phone, I noticed texts from a bunch of people that were useless, but Raj seemed to be persistent with trying to reach her, so I went to his messages.

Raj: I don't know where you are but get back to me

Raj: Ari listen I don't know if you mad that I brought Paris in the bedroom with us but trust I won't do it again

Raj: yo some dudes came here looking for you

Raj: if you don't answer me I'm going to tell Kori everything that you've done to take her down.

The last message piqued my interest. Looking through their messages, I wanted to see how she talked to him, so he wouldn't suspect anything.

Ari: what the fuck you want Raj

Raj: wow that's how you respond after you been gone for some days, you got niggas running up on me about shit you mixed up with and I gotta hide out now.

Ari: I'm not mixed up in this by myself you're a part of it

Raj: foh I didn't steal them drugs from Deuce, you did and now he want your ass!!

Shocked, I dropped the phone on the bed. Thinking quickly I text back

Ari: I'm good but what's that hot shit you talking about you telling Kori???

Raj: bitch you only think about yourself, you know you fucked up for selling Kori to him right, and what he gon do to her when he gets her doesn't scare you? What about her grandmother's death?

My head started spinning, thinking about what he could possibly do to me if he didn't get Ari instead. How could she give me up for him? How much drugs did she owe him for him to want me instead of his payout? What had she done to my grandmother? I knew I had to call Edo; he was the only person who could help me out at this point.

144

The Drop:

Looking down at my phone, I saw wifey flash across the screen. A smile spread across my face; instead of answering it, I had to send her to voicemail. I was meeting my uncle at this spot for a drop and he had yet to show up. Tempted to call Kori just to hear her voice, I didn't want to be off my A game and get caught up.

Shooting Diesel a text that I was at the spot in Queens, he responded:

why the fuck are you there we in the spot in the Bronx?

Raising my brow, I looked over the text my uncle sent and it said to meet him in Queens. Now, I was fed up cuz something didn't seem right with this drop. I was here with all the coke, no back up, and I left my gun in my car.

Jetting out the warehouse, it was surrounded by 3 police cars "Fuck!" I shouted as they came to arrest me. Shaking my head, they led me into the patrol car, reading me my rights. "Ain't this about a bitch. I was set up!" Hauling my ass to the bookings, all I could think about was Kori and if she was okay. I hadn't heard from her in a few weeks; I wanted her close to me. I missed the hell outta her little ass.

"Let's go." Placing me in the cell, they ended up giving me my phone call. I called my lawyer. "Yo Andrews, I been booked. I need you to get in touch with Diesel and get me out ASAP!"

"Okay Edo, I'm on it; we should be there shortly," he ended the call. Mad, I didn't call Kori, but I knew she wouldn't know what to do once I broke the news of being arrested to her.

Now, it was the waiting game, hoping I could get my ass outta here before I had to catch another case from one of these niggas trying me.

Kori

Unanswered calls:

Losing my mind, I tried calling Edo back to back, only to be sent to voicemail. This was not like him to block my calls. Maybe he had enough of my back and forth games and said to hell with me. Ari would be showing her face tomorrow for the weekend, and I was not prepared to deal with what I was just told. To add fuel to the fire, I had a baby in me to protect. After leaving Diesel a text about Edo not reaching out, he responded that he would make sure he got in touch with me. Feeling overwhelmed and sad, I cried myself to sleep thinking here it was I was pregnant by the man who had my heart, and I was alone in a different state waiting on my ex who sold me to her dealer to save her ass.

Chapter 32

Diesel

Hearing Edo got knocked was a smack in the face. I told Deuce what had transpired and the nigga had the nerve to say, "It is what it is." Aggravation and shock overcame me as I thought that this nigga set up his own nephew because Edo actually wanted out of the game. How could you hold a grown man hostage because you wanted to retire and go be the family man? Shit, at this point, I was ready to pass the torch too. I had more than enough saved for my kids and me and Kristen.

"Babe, so what are you going to do now?!" Kristen asked, as I thought about what Andrews said.

"He has no bail, he has to be arraigned and the judge can decide what the next step is." He shrugged and walked off.

"What the fuck they mean no bail? Edo wasn't the one in and out of juvies and prisons; he had a clean record so, unless they had him on a murder, why wasn't he set free?"

Looking over at Kristen, I saw the worry on her face and I contemplated continuing to deal with her if she couldn't understand this life. "Shit happens," I said, not trying to let Kristen know that I was just as clueless as her.

Shooting Marie a text and letting her know that Edo was locked up, she started calling me nonstop. "Auntie, if I knew the charges, then I could see what the holdup is," I stressed, trying to calm her down.

"But, what's really going on Diesel? Edo doesn't belong there and you and I both know this," she cried into the phone.

"Auntie, trust me, I'ma see what the deal is. Don't stress, I got this!" I tried to convince the both of us. Edo was always the one who was careful with how he handled shit. The only way all of this could have happened was if he was set up. In the past few months, Edo had gained some enemies after meeting Kori.

"Could she be behind all of this? I know a woman scorned is worst then your worst enemy," I said to no one in particular, as I left out to put my ear to the streets.

Chapter 33

Marie

An emotional wreck

"Andrews, what is going on with my nephew!" I yelled into the phone. "Get him out ASAP and you better not tell me you have no control over what they are doing!"

I waited on his response. "Listen Mrs. Samuels, you think if I couldn't get him out, I wouldn't," he said out of frustration.

"I don't know because clearly, you're not doing shit!" Letting the tears stain my face, I asked, "Where the fuck is my husband? Has he not contacted you about this?" I was trying to pull myself together.

"No, I haven't heard from him, Mrs. Samuels."

"Fine, I'll just have to see what is going on myself." Hanging up the phone in his ear, I was over the run around. Edo was the only child I raised, so I looked at him like a son. I raised him right, he graduated, and got a degree in business management because of me. If it was up to Deuce, he would just know how to run the blocks.

Hightailing to my lawyer's office, I walked right through the doors and straight to his office. "Miss," the receptionist called after me. Waving my hand in her direction, I continued until I got to his office, pounding on the door and not caring if he was on a call or with another client; I needed him right now. Swinging the door open just as the receptionist caught up to me, she looked over at him.

"I tried to stop her sir," she said, trying to catch her breath.

"Jada, it's okay. You will learn that she is one of my highest profile clients and, when she comes, everything else stops," he chuckled while looking me over. "Meet my new receptionist Jada, and this is Marie Samuels."

After the introductions, I walked in his office. Closing the door behind me, I made myself comfortable. I dropped my YSL bag on his oak desk. "Kaine, I need you!" I stressed.

"Baby, when don't you need me," he said, seductively licking his lips.

"No dammit, Kaine, I'm serious. My nephew was arrested and I need him out right now!"

Tapping his desk with my index finger, he said, "Come here," motioning me to step between his legs while he sat on the edge of his desk. Taking me in his embrace, I leaned on his chest and let out a sigh.

"That bastard set up my baby, I know he did."

"I been telling you for years, Marie, that your husband is one shady ass man and you have yet to believe me. Yet, you claim you trust me." Lifting my chin with his hand, he asked, "Look at me, do you not trust me, baby?"

Nodding my head, I knew this looked fucked up. Here it was I was married to Deuce, yet fucking one of the highest paid African American lawyers in NYC. It didn't start out like this. I came to Kaine 2 years ago because I found out that Deuce had cheated yet again. I wanted to draw up my own prenup, just in case I needed to protect myself during our divorce. In doing so, I ran into Kaine, who was a criminal lawyer. My lawyer, Mr. Torres, introduced us and, although I was hesitant to reach out to him, one day Deuce had put his hands on me and, from that day on, our relationship had changed.

I left Romero, my ex, because he was abusive, so it was no way I was going to allow this man to bring me back to this low place in my life.

Calling up Kaine, he met me for lunch and, after protesting, I agreed to link at his house to hide the busted lip Deuce had given me hours earlier because I disrespected him in front of Edo. After seeing my face, he made me promise him that if he had ever put his hands on me again, that I would leave. Although he didn't physically hit me, the verbal abuse started and the women started to multiply. I then started paying Kaine to help me and Edo out on the side.

"Kaine, they have Edo locked up in the bookings and he wasn't given bail, so I know he will be in court tonight." Sighing heavily, I sat on the sofa in his office. "I don't know but when I find out what part Deuce played in this, I'm going to kill him, and I need another favor babe." Looking down at the floor, I twiddled my fingers.

"Wassup Marie, you good?"

Hanging my head low in shame, "Can you help me find a good private investigator?" I asked, swallowing the lump in my throat.

"C'mon, you know that's not an issue; is everything else okay?" he quizzed, grabbing my feet and removing my shoes while resting them in his lap. Massaging my feet, I laid my head back, letting a low moan escape my lips. "You need to just let me take care of you, Marie." Moaning, he worked his way from my feet to my thighs. "I'm not just talking sexual babe, divorce that street thug you're with and allow me to treat you like the queen you are," he said, removing my panties from under my skirt.

Unable to think straight, I just nodded my head in agreement. "Okay Kaine but, for right now, just fuck me slow." Propping my leg up on his shoulder, Kaine kissed his way from my thighs to my love box. Throwing my head back in complete bliss, "Umm Kaine," I moaned. He kissed on my kitty, licked it and slowly sucked on my clit while I tried to muffle my moans, remembering we were in his office. Sticking two of his fingers inside of me sent me over the edge. "Fuck Kaine."

Grinding on his fingers as he continued to suck on my clit, I moaned, "Oh, my God, I'm cumming." Squeezing my legs tight around his head, I creamed on his chin. Kaine lapped up all my juices before going into his bathroom grabbing a small hand towel.

"Come home with me today," he said, wiping me off.

"Kaine, you know I would love to do that, but what if Deuce shows his face? What will I tell him?"

Watching his jaws clench at the mention of Deuce's name, "Fuck that nigga, Marie; he doesn't love you!" He spat.

I threw my underwear in my bag; at this point, I had no use for them. "Kaine, just give me a few more months and I promise I'll be yours," I pleaded.

"Marie, I'm telling you to leave before he takes you down with him. If he does that, I can only try to save you, ma." Sighing, I knew Kaine was right, but I couldn't leave just yet, not when Edo needed me most.

Hopping up from the sofa, I asked, "So, are you going to make the calls to see what's going on babe?" Wrapping my hands around his neck, I looked into his hazel eyes.

"Yea babe, give me about an hour to get back to you," he said, prying my hands from around him.

Sensing his change in attitude, I asked, "Kaine, what's wrong?"

"Marie, you know what's my problem. These games, I'm too old for them." Looking over in my direction, he looked out the window, turning his back to me. "Hell, you're too old for this shit. You're 15 years older than me and you acting immature."

Stunned by his straight forwardness, I looked at him; his back muscles flexed while he rubbed his hand across his chin. Kaine was so sexy, especially when he was mad. I admired everything about him from his 6'2" muscular frame to his toned legs and caramel complexion. "Fine Kaine, then don't help me." Throwing my hands up, I placed my feet in my red bottoms and scooped up my purse.

"Marie, don't do that!" he warned.

Yes, I was 15 years his senior, but he would not give me an ultimatum, when my life could be in danger if I walked away now. Placing my oversized Chanel glasses on my face, I retorted, "I'm out." Leaving out of his office and heading out the door, I noticed the receptionist staring in my direction.

"Have a great day!" she called out.

Swinging my bone straight hair over my shoulder, I waved. Once I got to my car, I checked to see I had 3 missed calls from my husband. Rolling my eyes, "Hey," I spoke dryly.

"You heard what happened to Edo?"

"Yea, I did Deuce. I'm surprised you're just calling me after all this damn time; where have you been?" I questioned with annoyance dropping from my voice.

"Bitch, have you lost your mind questioning me!" he barked. This was the Deuce I'd grown to hate; he was not the loving husband who took me away from my abusive ex. He was heartless and a complete alcoholic.

"I'm sorry baby, I was just worried about you," I mustered up to say.

"You better be, I'll be out of town for a few days. I'll keep in touch, don't be blowing up my line Marie!"

"Okay Deuce, I hear you" He ended the call with not as much as a I love you or nothing. Relieved that he was leaving, a smile spread across my face while sending Kaine a text

Marie: Kaine I'll be home by the time you get there

Kaine: I'm glad you came to your senses

Rolling my eyes at his cocky response, I didn't even bother replying. Hoping that when he came home he would have some answers for me, I headed straight to my house to pack an overnight bag.

Chapter 34

Jada

Watching the lady walk out of Kaine's office, something seemed very familiar about her. I didn't know if it was her features, her walk, or her voice, but I definitely been around her before. With only working in this new firm for all of two weeks, I didn't have the authority to ask Kaine who she was but, after he did give me her first name, I decided to look into her profile and see if anything about her seemed familiar. Pulling up the computer, I noticed there were a few Marie's logged in.

"Just my luck she has one of the most popular names there is," I said. Trying to go through all 15 Maries in the system without seeming suspicious would be hard because Kaine showed his face more than most of the lawyers I knew. He probably thought I wasn't hip to the fact that he just fucked the shit out of her in his office, so I knew she couldn't be one of the few that were married.

Damn near jumping out my skin, Kaine was staring in my direction. Hopping up, I asked, "Can I get you anything Sir?"

"Hold all my calls for the rest of the day. I'm leaving the office, I will see you in the morning Jada," he said while nodding and smiling as he walked away. "Oh and while you're probably looking for Marie's information in the system, you're not going to find it," he chuckled.

I was shocked. All I could manage to say was "Goodnight." Reaching for my phone to tell Kristen I was busted, I saw that Kori had sent me and Kristen a few messages in our group chat that she needed us.

Jada: sorry I'm late ladies, Kori are you okay?

Kori: bitch no, tf I said Edo is not answering my calls and I'm worried sick, literally

Jada: oh I'm sorry, well why not just go pop up at his house

Kori: because if he's in trouble then I could risk myself being in trouble as well

Jada: you right

Kristen: sorry guys but I haven't heard anything and neither has Diesel

Kori: ok thanks, love y'all bye

After telling Kori I'd check on her later, I couldn't help but to think Kristen was hiding something, and I was going to find out sooner or later.

Chapter 35

Kristen

"Babe, I don't understand why I can't just tell Kori that he's locked up," I whined.

"Kristen, because we don't know whose behind him getting locked up, damn!" he shouted, tossing his phone on the bed. "I told you to keep your mouth shut, this shit is not a game," he stressed.

"Okay fine." Rolling my eyes, I was growing tired of Diesel having me keep secrets from my sister. Yes, I wanted to protect her, but I also knew that she was hardheaded and, if she got a hunch about something, she was going to seek answers. "Have you asked your aunt about it?"

"Yes Kristen, what the fuck!" he shouted, grabbing his phone and keys. "I'm out. When you stop asking me shit, I'll be back yo." Leaving out, he slammed the door shut.

Oh, this nigga must think I'm one of his baby mamas, huh? He had another thing coming; I was the one doing the leaving.

Chapter 36

Edo

Finding out that I was denied bail fucked up my head. Looking around the courtroom that night, I spotted my aunt, Diesel and Paris there. Hoping to have locked eyes with Kori, Paris was the one standing there with tears streaming down her face. Kicking myself, I knew her knowing my charges would only bring me more drama in the long run. I mouthed to my aunt about Deuce, and she shrugged her shoulders. I noticed he nor Kristen was in tow, but I did spot a dude standing right next to my aunt in a brand new suit rubbing the small of her back. *The fuck?!* I thought to myself. Watching his posture and aura, he seemed to be a good dude and I was a good judge in character.

Hearing the judge tell me the charges against me included possession of a large amount of crack cocaine, I knew I was going down when I saw it was a white female judge. I was trying to understand why my lawyer wasn't present after I paid him large amounts of cash to keep me informed of any police activity; he had nerve to not show face.

"Mr. Samuels, did you hear me?" the judge questioned while looking in my direction.

"No, can you repeat that please?"

"I said you will be held in the Greene Correctional Facility until your court date next month."

Sighing heavily, I ran my tongue across my teeth and shook my head. Being escorted out, my aunt had tears running down her face. Signaling that I was going to call her, she nodded in approval. Looking over at Paris, I rolled my eyes and, for a minute, I thought I saw the bitch grinning.

Diesel shook his head. Passing a note to my public defender, he turned to me. "Diesel gave me Kori's number for you." Smiling on the inside, I couldn't wait to hear her voice. At this moment, that's the only thing that would calm me down from spazzing out.

Chapter 37

Kori

The tears just won't stop falling

After not being able to reach Edo, I was a nervous wreck. Ari was here working my last nerve and, with me having the information I had, I needed to keep my distance from losing my cool. I was happy when she told me she was stepping out to handle something. I didn't put up a fight or try to keep her here; I actually wanted her gone. She was making me sick to my damn stomach and I was sure my baby growing inside of me was just as sick of her as I was. Looking at my phone, I saw that I had an incoming call from a number I didn't recognize. Against my better judgement, I decided to answer it anyway.

The Present:

"You have a prepaid call from, "Edo," at The Greene Correctional Facility. This call may be monitored or recorded for quality purposes." Hearing the automated machine end the message, I was eager to hear from the love of my life.

"Wassup mami," Edo spoke into the phone, causing my heart to swell.

Smiling from ear to ear, I replied, "Hey papi."

"Sup witchu, you miss a nigga?"

"Edo, you know I miss you, so stop talking foolish." Sitting on the white chaise that sat in the middle of my She-shed, I got comfortable as I listened to the man I'd grown to love over the past few months.

"Where that bitch at?" Edo asked.

Peeking up, I knew it was only a matter of minutes before he brought her up. Hearing the venom in his voice, I reassured him I was alone. "Papi relax, you have my undivided attention. I miss you tho, and I want to see you so bad!" Soothing him.

"So, make it happen ma. Don't talk about it, be about it."

After 15 minutes, I heard the familiar keys jingle. I knew it was none other than Ari. "Baby, I have to go."

"You have 2 minutes left," the automated voice said.

"Kori, you better not end this call before the machine say my time is up," he chastised.

Looking up, I figured I had better think fast if I didn't want her to hear me talking to Edo. Jumping up to close and lock the door, she appeared, pushing her way in. Dropping the phone in a panic, I heard Edo's voice booming through the speaker.

"Hey, baby girl."

Realizing my phone was still on a call, Ari picked up the phone, looking at the number that. Turning on her heels and placing the phone to her ear, "Didn't I say to stay away from my bitch? Your days are numbered Edo, try me if you want to while I got you by your balls," she spat.

"Bitch, you got me fucked-," the call ended.

Looking up at Ari with pleading eyes, she rushed to my side, yoking me up. "You got me fucked up if you think I'ma let you talk to this nigga like ain't nothing wrong!" she spat.

"Please Ari, it's not that serious!" Getting out of her grasp, I had to think about my unborn baby who deserved a fighting chance through all of this. Running and grabbing up my phone, I made it to the bathroom.

Locking the door while out of breath, I examined my neck in the mirror. With my hands shaking, I was able to send my location to the group chat I was in with Kristen and Jada.

Hearing the banging on the bathroom door brought me out of my trance. "Think Kori," I chastised, deciding to call the police.

"911, what's your emergency?" the operator said.

"I'm being attacked by my girlfriend. She choked me and I'm hiding in the bathroom. I'm pregnant and she's a police officer," I pleaded.

"Bitch, you called the cops on me!" Ari shouted "How dare you?! I'm going to kill you Kori!" Ari started beating the door down with her fist. "Open the fucking door!"

Standing up against the wall, I was looking at the door being hit. I searched to see if there was something I could use as a weapon if I needed to.

"Ma'am, what's your location?" the operator asked

"206 N Academy Ave." I ran off the address to the small apartment we were renting in PA. "Please hurry," I cried.

"Yo Kori, open the fucking door!" She stopped beating on the door. Feeling the vibration of my phone, Kristen and Jada both assured they were on their way to me, but it would take them a few hours before they reached the house.

Sighing, I noticed the towel holder. Taking it apart, I held the stick in my hand as tight as I could. "Ari, if you keep fucking with me, I'm going to beat your ass!" I spat. I had enough of her bullying bullshit for the last damn time.

"Oh, you growing some balls cuz you called the cops, you forgot I'm the fucking cops!"

"And your fucking point?!" Hearing the sirens in the background, I smiled a little. "Let's see your junkie ass weasel your way through this bitch!"

Ari charged through the bathroom door, falling into the bathtub. Thanking God that I moved to the side just in time, I ran out the bathroom just as the cops was breaking through the apartment. Guns raised, they screamed, "Drop the stick and put your hands up!"

Doing as I was told, I waited until one of them grabbed me while Ari was coming to the front. "She beat me and I'm pregnant!" I shouted before they tried to side with her.

One of the officers restrained Ari. "I'm a fucking cop; she's a fucking liar!" The officers looked from me to Ari.

"She is a cop, but she put her hands on me and she's a coke head. She's from the 40th Precinct in the Bronx." I'd be damned if I let her get away with this so she could have a chance to beat my ass again. After they took her in the car, one of the officers asked if I wanted to go to the hospital. I obliged, just to check to see if my baby was okay.

Chapter 38

Paris

Calling Deuce for what seemed like for hours, he finally answered. "Bitch, what the fuck you want?!"

"Deuce, don't hang up!" I pleaded. "I'm pregnant and it's yours."

Hearing him breathe heavily on the phone, "You got some nerve, you better handle that shit," I heard him say.

"Yo boss, I think I know where Kori is," I heard someone say.

"Hello Deuce," I said in almost a whisper.

"You still on my line, I just said handle that shit!"

"I need money to do so Deuce, or your little wife will just have to find out about us."

Chuckling, he said, "You threatening me, bitch? You forgot I know where you stay."

"No, but I also know that you're looking for Ari and Kori and I know where they are," I said, hoping he would take the bait.

"Bitch, stop playing with me, cuz I'm not the one for the games!" he spat.

I bet that caught his attention. "I'm serious." Hoping he would take me up on my offer, I waited.

"I'ma call your ass in a few days and you better pick up your damn phone Paris!" he roared.

"Fine." Ending the call, I was satisfied that he going to let me deliver Ari and Kori to him. Not really wanting to give up Ari, I was praying that he went during the week so she would be at the rehab center and catch Kori off guard, which would eliminate not only the problem I had with him but also then I could have Edo to myself again. At this rate, he was going to need all the support he could get.

Chapter 39

Raj

Devil's Advocate:

Putting in my two weeks' notice days ago was just what I needed to do for a while. Ari had me mixed up in a bunch of drama that I wasn't going to deal with. Looking at my blinking phone as I packed the last thing in my car, I saw I had a Facebook notification. Reading over the message, it was from Kori

Kori: hey sorry I didn't get back to you faster but I know what Ari did I was texting you in place of her a few days ago, she's been arrested because she put her hands on me. I'm in PA and I honestly need to be able to get back to NYC without anyone coming after me.

Rereading the message, I didn't know if I should respond or just ignore it and leave all that Ari drama alone.

Raj: I'm sorry you're going through this but I can't help you, I quit the force and I'm moving

Sending the message, I put my phone back in my pocket. Closing my trunk, I turned to leave. I felt a burning sensation in my chest. Looking down, I saw the blood pouring from my wound. Grabbing my chest, I looked up across the street and saw him staring at me with a smile on his face. It was one of the goons Deuce sent after me a few weeks ago. Rushing over to me, they picked me up and dragged me back into my apartment. Fearing the worst, I silently prayed until I looked up and noticed Deuce.

"I thought I sent some guys to tell you to bring me Ari a while ago. See, you been playing with me Raj and, although I want to kill you right now, I need you to do me a favor before you do." I shook my head. "I know you know how to get in touch with Kori and Ari. I need you to tell them to meet you here, it's urgent," he spat.

Pulling out my phone, I did as I was told and gave Kori my home address to meet me here. Before I could tell him it was done, he raised the gun and sent two more bullets into my chest.

Kori: ok Raj I'll be there tomorrow, thanks

Deuce smiled, thinking this was easier than he expected.

Chapter 40

Edo

"I swear, if something happens to Kori, Ari is going to wish I was dead," I mumbled., trying to call Kori back after the phone line went dead. I had no idea where the hell Kori was or if I could get someone to get in touch with her. With Kristen not showing up for my court date, I didn't know if they were on the outs again or not. Finding out the dude who was with my aunt was a criminal lawyer, I asked to get in contact with him. Being called to the room saying I had a visitor, I knew it had to be him because it was unexpected.

"Hello Mr. Samuels, how can I help you?" he asked.

"First of all, tell me your history with my aunt and then I'll see if you are more help than you are a threat!" I said, getting straight to the point.

"No doubt, my name is Kaine and I'ma criminal lawyer in New York. I met your aunt a few years ago by accident; she was meeting with one of my partners and we were introduced. She wanted to sign a prenup against your uncle."

174

Taking everything in, I noticed his tone change when he spoke about my aunt. "You fucking her?"

Caught off guard by my question, "C'mon Edo, do you really want to know that?" he asked.

"I asked, right?"

Sitting back in his chair, he responded, "Yea, we are engaging in sexual acts. What does that have to do with anything?"

"It has everything to do with it. Don't get my aunt mixed up in no bullshit because you had a taste of her pussy; my uncle is a dangerous man and I'm sure he would waste no time sparing you your life," I warned.

"Just like he had no problem sparing you yours, right?" he countered back.

Thinking about the fly shit he just said out his mouth, "What you said?" I asked, as if I didn't hear him.

"Listen, I know you don't want to believe what I gotta say cuz you don't know me, but I've been doing my research and, so far, all leads points to your uncle. Now, I don't have the concrete proof to get him booked, but I'm sure he's behind it all."

He handed me a folder. I immediately opened it and saw pics of Diesel and Deuce meeting up on numerous occasions, as well and phone records showing the activity between them. Looking at one picture in particular, I saw that it was the day I was busted. Deuce and Diesel were in the office in the Bronx. I knew because I had just left Diesel that day to meet my uncle in Queens. He had on the full outfit I remember him wearing. "So, now what?"

"I'm building my case against him and your old lawyer, for that matter. I needed to know if you think I should look at Diesel as a possible accomplice as well?" he suggested.

"I hope that's not necessary, but just keep a close eye out on him though." Finishing up the meeting between Kaine, I said, "Aye, don't hurt my aunt and keep her safe but, before you go, I need you to see if you can find my wife. Don't tell my aunt I'm asking you to do this; she hasn't met her yet. Her name is Koriann Mendez and goes by Kori; she has a sister named Kristen."

Nodding his head, he took the information I had on Kori and left. Feeling optimistic, I was ready to get out of here, so I could step to my uncle like a grown man and see what part Diesel was playing in this.

Chapter 41

Kristen

When the tables turn

Diesel thought I was playing when I sent him a text that I was leaving. Between the baby mama drama and him keeping secrets from me and everyone else, I was not sticking around while he brought us down. He thought I was stupid, but I knew about the secret meeting between him and Deuce and, next thing we know, Edo was locked up and caught with a drug charge. I remembered that night like it was yesterday. Diesel's work phone started ringing early in the morning; he rolled over, looking at the caller and exiting the room. If it were Edo, he would have taken the call in the room, so now that had my attention. Hearing him downstairs, I crept outta the bed and listened through the door.

"What you mean we're having a meeting without him? Deuce, c'mon now, Edo is family; why we excluding him?" Gasping, I held my hand over my mouth "Aight fine, I'll meet with you, even though I think this shit a lil funny." Diesel paused for a minute. "Oh word, you going to leave the empire to me? I thought you planned on giving it to Edo. Aight, aight I see your point." He ended the call.

I hurried to the bed to act like I was sleep. That was all I needed to hear, and then see that Edo was locked up just confirmed that Diesel was out for himself.

I packed while he was gone. I wanted to leave and not have to explain shit to him. Once I left, I blocked his numbers from contacting me and headed straight to Jada's house. I thanked God he didn't know where she lived, being she had moved and started a new job. When Kori reached out to the both of us telling us she needed us to get to her as soon as possible, we dropped everything and headed to the location she sent. Not understanding why the hell she was in PA, I dismissed the attitude that I felt brewing. Being Kori's older sister and protector since our grandmother's death, I had to drop everything and run to her aid.

"Do you know anything going on with Kori? Like why she sent the location?" Jada asked me.

"Jada, if I had all the answers, I wouldn't be speeding through the fucking highway trying to get my sister. Fuck, just shut up and take the ride!" I was aggravated that I couldn't do 100 on the highway and having Jada in my ear asking all these questions. I didn't know what I was stepping into. Edo was locked up and I didn't trust Diesel or Deuce, so here I was a going to save my sister with no clue as to how?

"Damn, I'm just asking because I could of told my boss and he could of possibly helped us out Kristen!" Jada frantically said.

Zoning her out, I thought of all the predicaments I could of been walking into. Was Kori hurt? Did she hurt Ari? Did she just need me to hold her?

"Kristen, do you hear me talking to you?"

"No, I don't Jada, what?" I turned my attention to her and off the road.

"I said maybe you should call Diesel and see if he can meet us there."

Sucking my teeth, I said, "Bitch, are you dumb?" Cocking my head to the side, I continued, "I told you I don't trust that nigga and I refuse to call him and let him know my sister's situation, when he could possibly be behind Edo getting knocked!" I gritted my teeth, "So, like I said, if you're riding, pull your ass together or I can drop your ass off right here in jersey!"

Falling back into the passenger seat sighing, Jada stressed, "You know I'm riding. Listen, I'll fight a bitch in a heartbeat for any one of you, but I will not fuck with no chick who could shoot me and I don't have no gun."

Understanding where she was coming from, I nodded and continued driving. When the GPS alerted that we were only 15 minutes from the destination, I told Jada to reach out to Kori. After her phone continued to go to voicemail, Jada started panicking. "Kris, what if she's not okay? What if she is dead?" Jada cried.

Popping Jada on her thigh, I retorted, "Don't you say that shit again until you know for sure Jada!" Pulling the car over, I decided to call Kori until she finally answered in almost a whisper.

"Kris, are you coming to get me?" she cried into the phone.

"Yes baby, I'm close. I'm like 15 minutes away," I reassured her.

"Kris, I'm in the hospital. I'ma send you the location. Just please hurry, my phone is cracked and dying."

Hearing her voice crack broke me down. Hanging up while waiting on her message, I let all my tears fall. "Kris, what did she say?! Kris!" Jada shrieked.

"She's in the hospital. I don't know what's wrong; I just know she's there." Noticing I was less than 5 minutes from the hospital, I sped down the next three blocks.

Entering the hospital, I tried sending Kori messages and calling her. Realizing her phone must have died, I asked the receptionist if she had her checked in. Once they told me she was discharged, I was relieved. "Okay, what unit was she in?"

Looking at the monitor again, she replied, "She was treated in the emergency room 1C3."

Thanking her, I ran towards that way with Jada in tow. "So, she's okay if she was discharged then, Kristen. Stop worrying."

Turning to face Jada, I stressed, "Listen, that little girl is my heart. I raised her when our mother dropped us off so, as long as I'm breathing and walking this earth, I will worry about her!" Glaring over Jada's shoulder, I saw Kori speed walking my way. Pulling her into an embrace,

Kori cried until she had no tears left in her. Jada rubbed her back while I just held her.

"I have to go. I have to get back to the city before they let Ari go. She's locked up but I don't, I don't know for how long because-"

Raising my hand, I cut her off. "Let's just get you back to New York; we can talk about it later." Showing her to the car, she asked that we stop at the small apartment Ari was renting for them out there.

"Edo is locked up," she stressed, falling into the back.

"I know sis, I'll tell you all about that tomorrow. Tonight, you just need to rest." Jada was silent for the most part. "So, you have nothing to talk about now?" I asked her.

"I mean, I'm just worried about this relationship between Kori and Ari," she spoke up.

Kori popped her head up from the backseat. "There is no Ari and me. I want to be with Edo; I just have to be able to see him," she cried again. Once we were at the apartment, we grabbed as much of Kori's belongings as we could. Noticing the door was broken in the bathroom and the items that was disarray, I knew Kori had finally fought back. Kori went to use the restroom when I saw the picture in her purse. Holding it up, I showed it to Jada, whose eyes lit up with excitement. Kori came out the bathroom looking from me and Jada.

"Oh yea, I'm expecting." She smiled weakly with tear filled eyes.

"Aww Boobie, I'ma be a god mommy." Jada rushed to her stomach, rubbing her belly.

"I'm not too far along and didn't want to tell y'all until I knew how the baby was doing."

"Well, how is my niece or nephew?" I asked.

"I'm 13 weeks and the baby is healthy, despite the abuse." Hanging her head low, she asked, "Can we leave?" Looking over at Kori, I could see the pregnancy taking a toll on her body. Her face was pale and her boobs looked bigger than usual; I couldn't see a belly because she had on a sweatshirt. Her eyes looked tired and her once tamed hair was pulled up in a messy bun, not the ones that's cute either.

"Yes, let's get you to the house so you can sleep." The drive back to NYC was smoother than coming out here. Jada was driving and Kori was snuggled in my lap in the back seat. Between looking out the window and looking down at a sleeping Kori, I was relaxed for the most part.

"Jada, she is not to leave away from us."

"You don't have to tell me that. She's pregnant and I know Ari's ass doesn't know or Kori would be dead." Once we made it back to Jada's apartment, we talked for a few until Kori said she was so exhausted, which I could only imagine.

"Oh tomorrow, I need to go to the Ari's partner house. I heard y'all talking about don't let me outta y'all sight, I'm fine." She turned on her heels "I'm not a baby and I love you both, but this is something I have to do alone and I'll explain everything to y'all when I get back."

Chapter 42

Diesel

Prove your loyalty:

I'd been beating myself up for the past few days, not just because Edo was locked up but Kristen had left me without as much as a goodbye. I knew I was hard on her the last time we were talking, but she had to understand I was just as clueless and worried as she was. How could I tell her that I figured Deuce had something to do with Edo's arrest without it looking like I was just as shady? When Deuce told me to meet him in the spot in the Bronx, I had just left Edo and, instead of replaying the conversation me and Deuce had days prior, I bounced without telling him anything.

Deuce felt like Edo was a threat to him when it came to handling the streets. Although Edo had been in the streets since he was young, Edo wanted out and wanted to go legit with a few businesses. Once he met Kori, he kept telling me, "She's the one bro, I'ma make her my wife and leave this game alone." Knowing he had the record label to fall back on, he was tired of the street shit.

Checking Edo's visitor's schedule, I was relieved to see he didn't revoke me rights to go check on him. I had to let him know what was up, although I didn't know the full ins and outs of Deuce's actions. I did know Edo had a right to know his uncle wasn't playing fair and his freedom was in his hands.

Calling up Andrews to see why he wasn't taking the case, I was met with his voicemail. *This nigga picked a fine time to start going missing* was all I could think about as I took the drive to Greene. Trying to call Kristen once more, the call didn't go through. I wasn't one to chase a bitch, but it was something special about Kristen and I was sure the same about Kori; that's why my nigga was open.

Entering the jail, I passed through the security and waited for Edo to show his face. Looking up at him walking through the door, he didn't look too stressed. Trying to read his body language, I came up empty handed. "Sup bruh," I greeted him. Edo just nodded and sat down across from me.

"What you doing here Diesel? You know we don't visit no jails," he asked.

"C'mon bro, you know I had to come check on ya; this shit is nasty and you shouldn't be here."

"I'm glad you figured that shit out. What the fuck happened that night I left you?" he asked through gritted teeth.

Looking down at the gray table and back at him, I responded, "Bro, I don't-"

Edo hit the table. "Diesel, don't fix your mouth to lie to me yo, and don't bro me when you doing some fuck shit!"

I shook my head in anger. "Listen, I don't know what happened after I left you, but I know I was sent a message to meet Deuce yo in the Bronx at the spot."

"Nigga, you knew I said I had to head to the queens warehouse to link with Deuce; you ain't realize no shady shit then?"

I looked at Edo as if he was crazy "Yo, you think I set you up?!" I was shocked by his accusations.

"Nigga, who the fuck else did but you and Deuce? You running around with that nigga like the shit don't look like a set up!"

Seeing his point, I couldn't even argue with him for thinking I was foul. "Listen, I had nothing to do with that shit. Trust me when I say it." I decided I should just come clean and tell him about the offer Deuce presented to me.

"Yo, where Andrews been?" he asked.

"I don't know. I been calling him to see why he missed your court date but, on the real tho Edo, we go way back and you always held me down through everything, so I can't sit here and withhold this deal Deuce was trying to spit to me."

Edo looked over at me with a sinister look. "Speak on it then."

"Deuce planned on leaving me as the next boss in charge." I was trying to be as careful with my words. "He said something to the effect of you not showing that you really about this street shit."

Edo stared at me. "How long you knew this?"

"Not too long but, when I planned to tell you, that's when you got knocked." He shook his head.

"So, as of right now, I don't trust you, my nigga. I do know that Kori is in some trouble and I need to get in touch with her. Shit, I need to see her."

I took in everything that Edo said. "Nah, no doubt I'll get in touch with her. What you want to do about this Deuce situation?"

"You decide, prove to me where your loyalty lies," and with that, the guard told us his visit was up.

Leaving out, I didn't have the slightest clue as to how I was going to handle Deuce but, once Edo ran off Kori's number, I plugged it in my phone to give her a call.

"Hey, can I ask whose calling?" she spoke into the phone.

"Yo Kori, it's Diesel. I need to link with you as soon as possible; are you free?"

"Not right now, a little later I am. I can come by your house if that's okay with you?"

"Yea, no doubt, around what time?" The phone went silent for a while.

"Around 4 I should be free."

I started up the car. "Aight bet, Edo wants to see you too, so we gotta make that happen."

"I wanna see him too. I miss him so much."

Hearing the cracking in her voice, I asked, "You good sis?"

"Yea, I just miss him, that's all."

Sensing she was lying to me, I said, "Kori, I hope you're not lying to me."

"Diesel, he doesn't know, but I'm pregnant and I'm scared to tell him. I saw he called me earlier when I was getting my phone fixed, so you think he will accept the baby being that he's locked up?" she asked.

"Yea sis, he gon accept that shit. That nigga love your little ass and you carrying his baby sis; he about to put your ass on lock down"

Chuckling, she started laughing. "Okay fine, so I'm going to handle what I have to and then come see you."

"Copy and be safe, your secret is safe with me." Hanging up, I was excited Kori was expecting. Hopefully getting her and Edo back together would help me and Kristen out cuz I missed her ass something terrible. Sending Kori over a message, I told her to bring Kristen along with her to my house and she agreed. I couldn't wait til Edo heard this news.

Chapter 43

Deuce

Hearing that Edo was locked up was great news and, now having Diesel on my side, I was sure I was going to be able to live the life I deserved, make the money while not doing the work, and keeping my record company as well. I knew Edo wanted out. I felt it in his lack of attention he was paying to the shipments and deals. After taking care of Raj, I was steps closer to get Kori and eventually have Ari killed. Paris was another problem; she was playing a deadly game and, at this point, I couldn't take any shit from anybody. Her threatening to tell Marie about us was more than I needed right now. Marie was not only my wife but she also was my partner in Diamond Records, so losing my wife to this ratchet bitch was not something I was willing to take. If I had to cut the damn baby outta her myself and watch her bleed to death, I would. Paris knew that when me and her started fucking around that it was just a fuck; she swore Edo was going to wife her up and that ship had sailed. Finding out he was dealing with Kori, who Ari adored, made it way more easier to track her sexy ass down.

At first, I was going to fuck with Ari by snatching up Kori and threatening her until Ari came out of hiding to kill her for disrespecting me but, when I could fuck with two people, I couldn't stand by. I was snatching her up, then I was definitely going to enjoy having Kori.

Call me sick or whatever but, when someone fucked with me, I always told them to pray that I didn't find out it was them or I wasn't alive cuz if I was, they would be sorry. Yeah, I was shady for turning Diesel on Edo but, as Edo got older, I saw a lot of his grimy father in him and the sight of him started to disgust me. Lorenzo had my sister caught up in a lot of shit, due to him treating people like shit and shitting on them and only looking out for self. I had Andrews promise he wouldn't take none of Edo's calls or go to his court dates or he would have to answer me and, as much dirt as I had on him, he fell back and stayed out of sight. Having Kori meet me at Raj's house was going to work in my favor because she thought she was going to find out info about Ari and nobody would ever suspect anything foul, which would clean my trail and get ghost quick.

As I waited for her arrival, I thought of how Marie was acting uninterested last night when I came home. She claimed she wasn't feeling good, but I knew her better than she thought. Something was bothering her and I would soon find out what it was. Yes, I had cheated from time to time, but Marie knew I would never have a chick disrespect her or make her feel like she had anything over her. I was a man that had needs and, when I wanted to be fucked by a slut, I refused to allow my wife to let me manhandle her in the bedroom. So, in return, I found chicks to do that and ended up passing them off to the highest bidder.

Hearing the car out front, I jumped up from the sofa. I sat on and told my two men to get ready for showtime. I heard Kori's voice on the phone as she got closer to the house. "I'm coming over right after I told her to meet me there, even tho she wasn't too happy," she chuckled. Noticing she was touching the knob, the door was unlocked. "Hold on, let me call you right back."

The apartment was dark. I could see her from the light that shined through the window, but she couldn't see me. Once she was fully in the apartment, the first thing she noticed was the blood. "What the fuck?!" She bent over, throwing up all over the living room.

Damn, she got a weak ass stomach I thought as I watched her trying to pull herself together. Instructing my man to come from the closet and grab her, she screamed before he covered her mouth to shut her up. Showing my face, she looked scared as hell; damn, she was beautiful.

"If you scream again, I'm goin to have my man shut you up. Now, I'm trying to not restrain your little pretty ass, but don't test me little girl!" I demanded. She stared directly in my eyes. I expected her to cry, but she didn't; she just looked at me with much attitude. "Now, you're going to come with me but, before I take you to have some fun, I need that phone."

Dropping her phone out of her hand, I smashed it, cracking her screen. "Bring her over here. Now Kori, if you give me a hard time, you're going to end up like your buddy Raj over there." She followed my eyes and saw his lifeless body in the corner. Opening her mouth, she puked once more, all over her and my mans. He tossed her to the floor.

"The fuck boss, this bitch can't hold shit down." Looking down at her on the floor angered me.

"Nigga, didn't I tell you before she got here that she is not to be handled roughly unless I gave you the orders to do so!"

"Nigga, she threw up on me. What the fuck was I supposed to do!"

"Pick her up and bring her to the damn van."

Her eyes got big as he dragged her. "I can walk, you don't have to drag me nigga!" she spat. I found the shit funny cuz not only was she sexy, but she was feisty too.

"Bitch!"

"Yo Tony, just let her walk. I'm sure she ain't running nowhere."

Rolling her eyes, she got in the backseat. "Where the fuck you taking me? I know you're Deuce, but guess what? The money that bitch Ari owe you, you're not getting cuz the hoe is locked up!" She shrugged. "So, let me go. I don't have nothing to do with that bullshit" l

Looking back at her, I smiled wickedly. "You may not have anything to do with the money, but you have everything to do with Ari and Edo!" Looking at the horror on her face, she turned away to look out the window.

When we made it to Queens, Kori was up against the backseat door. She hadn't said a word since I told her and she wasn't trying to look in me or my man's face. Opening up the door, I told him to blindfold her so she wouldn't know exactly where we were. Kori squirmed. "Bitch, don't try to break free of his grasp."

"You're hurting me dammit," she said as he dragged her in the house.

"Put her up in the first room. I'll be back for her in a minute."

Turning to face him, I said, "Don't do anything stupid either yo." He nodded, leaving me to myself.

What the hell have they gotten me into?

Blindfolded and manhandled was not how I wanted to be treated while I was pregnant. I was starving, but I wouldn't tell that scumbag Deuce. Whatever plans he had for me, I had to hold it down like Edo would want. If it was information he wanted, he had another thing coming. I knew nothing about Edo's operation or Ari's drug using or selling. I was really green to this shit and I needed to not show my fear, for my little nugget's sake.

When he tossed me down onto the floor, I knew I had made it to the first room, as Deuce said. Hearing faint screams in the background from a female, I could only imagine what was going on. "Don't take that shit off until you hear the door locked or I'll put a bullet in your head bitch!" he spat. Cocking my head to the side, I couldn't help but to think

197

about what Deuce said about him not touching me. Maybe I could play them against each other and get my ass up outta here.

Hearing the door lock, I took the blindfold off so fast to look at my surroundings. Noticing that the room was huge and, from what it looked like, it was clean. I immediately took off my Apple Watch and cut it on. Noticing all the text I had, I thought, *damn, this shit is not going to last long.* Thinking quickly, I sent a message to Diesel.

Kori: he got me, in house, Deuce, Queens

Diesel: what the fuck Kori? What are you saying?

Kori: no phone only watch can't talk much, location?

My heart was beating rapidly as I tried to keep an eye out on the doorway to notice any feet.

Diesel: yea

Sending Diesel the location and telling him bye so I could hide my watch in a safe place once I cut it off, I prayed he made to me before this dude did anything to me. Stripping out of my sweat shirt that had puke on it, the door swung open, scaring me half to death. Holding my chest, I moved up against the wall. When the lights turned on, I was shocked to see it was Diesel's baby mother, Rochelle, staring back at me.

"Boss man said to put this on after you shower." She tossed the shorts and tank pj set to me. She looked at me. "Kristen?!" She raised her brow, shaking my head no.

"Kori," I whispered.

She walked closer. "Edo's girl?" Nodding my head stepping back from her, I didn't know what to expect being I'd heard about the drama between her and my sister. "Why are you here?" she questioned in almost a whisper.

"I could ask you the same thing," I spat.

"I work for Deuce. I clean up the women; now, why are you here?"

Shrugging, I said, "I guess he wants to teach Ari and Edo a lesson."

She gasped. "Girl, I gotta get you outta here if it's what I think." Hearing movement outside of the bedroom door, she said, "Listen, do as he says. I'ma see about getting you outta here, even if I have to tell my baby father about this."

I raised my eyebrow. "He doesn't know you work here?"

She shook her head no and went to leave out. "Don't upset boss man, okay."

She left out and I was happy I had someone who had my back in here. Stepping into the bathroom, I showered, scrubbing all the throw up residue off my skin. Once I was finished bathing and washing my hair, I washed out my clothes. *I'll be damned if I didn't have a clean outfit to wear when I got out of this place*, I thought to myself. Putting on the pjs that was obviously too small for me, my perky breasts were spilling out of the top of it, fitting snug against my round belly that I tried to hide. The shorts stopped at the cuff of my butt, looking more like boy shorts than house shorts. Post baby weight, this set would look more like pajamas than a tank and underwear set. Rubbing my small stomach, "I'ma get us out of here baby," I said, talking to my belly as I had been doing ever since I found out I was pregnant.

Stepping into the room, I admired the décor. The room was lavish; it was adorned with a king bed, dresser with mirror, nightstand, chest dresser, and a chaise. The color scheme was a soft blue and gray with a plush faux fur rug in front of the bed. Hearing a knock on the door, I hopped in the bed, shielding my body from the intruder.

"Relax baby girl, it's just daddy," Deuce said, taking in the smell. "I like your hair wet; you're so beautiful. No wonder them two knuckleheads been causing a ruckus over you." He chuckled, but I didn't see a damn thing funny "I know you're wondering what you're doing here, huh?!"

Rolling my eyes while flaring my nose at him, I retorted, "You think?!"

Walking over to me, he sat on the bed a little too close for comfort. I moved back.

"Stop being so feisty ma. I'm not going to hurt you unless you want me to." He leaned in,touching my damp curls and pushing them from my face. "I just wanna admire you for a bit, you have this glow about you."

Breathing heavily, "Don't touch me, bastard!" I spat, which obviously pissed him off.

He pushed me, pinning me against the headboard. "You will not disrespect me. I'm trying to treat you better than I treat the rest of these bitches in here but, if you want their treatment, I can take ya ass down to the cold basement!"

Looking me over with hungry eyes, he stopped at my baby bump that I so hard tried to suck in. "Stand up," he ordered. Doing as I was told, I stood up away from him, using that as my cue to put some space between us. "Are you pregnant?!" he asked, which sounded more like a statement than a question. Not sure how to answer it, I looked away from his glare. "I take that as a yes." Smiling, he said, "I'ma have fun with that wet pussy, pregnant pussy is the best." He rubbed his hand across his chin. I swallowed hard, hoping he would have showed me some mercy because I was with child. He went and locked the door.

"I know you're a freak, you done been with a female and male, so don't act like you scared of this dick either." Deuce walked over to me, pushing me on the bed. Letting out a low scream, he decided to have his way with me. From ripping the pj set off, to him putting me up in any and every position he wanted me to be in. When he rammed his hard big dick in me, I thought I was going to pass out. Feeling my stomach get hard, I knew it was only a matter of time before he fucked me so hard that he would kill my baby.

He screamed out, "So you like fucking my nephew huh, he fuck you like this or like that!"

I was turned completely off. *Sick bastard*, I thought. Just when I thought he was finished as he announced himself cumming, he told me to open my mouth and catch his cum. *Oh, hell no, this nigga must be dumb if he think I'm doing that*, I thought as he jerked his dick til it went limp, shooting cum all over me. He looked down and saw I didn't catch the semen and slapped me across my face, sending me flying down to the mattress.

"Bitch, when I say drink my cum, you do that shit!" Getting up, he pulled up his boxers and pants before removing his belt and striking me with it. Screaming out in pain, I tried to back away until I hit the headboard. "You lucky I need to get this video done or I'd whip your ass until the white meat showed!" Raising up to leave the room, he said, "Get your ass cleaned up and I'll have one of these bitches bring you downstairs." Hearing him call Rochelle, I was a little relieved. "Get that disrespectful bitch cleaned up!"

She came running in, looking me over. Trying to get up from the bed, my legs and kitty was sore. Noticing the spots of dried up blood on the sheets, I prayed my baby was fine but, after being fucked in my ass and pussy, I didn't think I would even last through the night with all the pain.

"Oh, my God, let me help you, Kori. I texted Diesel and he said he was coming, so I'm going to try to get you outta here." As she lifted me to walk to the bathroom, I fell and balled up in pain; the cramps I felt in my stomach was excruciating enough to kill me. "C'mon Kori, you have to try hun."

Crying, I said, "I think he killed my baby." Shivering, I was a nervous wreck.

Her eyes widened. "You're pregnant, does he know?"

"Yes." Sighing heavily, Rochelle brought me to the bath and washed me up, then dressed me.

"Just do as he say Kori," she stressed after she did my makeup and hair, making me change into this red baby doll lingerie with a sheer robe to go over it. Giving me the one over, she said, "Ok, you look great. Just let them guys take pictures of you,but try not to get outta line. He will fuck you up worst Kori."

Nodding in approval, I thought *God, why are you doing this to me?*

Entering the basement, I saw a line of women, good looking women, fly bodies, hair and makeup done all dressed in lingerie, leaning up against the wall. On the opposite side, there was a man with a camera rolling and a projector behind him, showing 5 men around a table with cards. "What the fuck is this shit?" Hearing them call these women by their names, the women stepped up one by one posing for pictures. One would think they enjoyed it by the way they flaunted their bodies but, looking at their faces, I saw the horror in their eyes. The men shouted, lifted up cards with numbers on it, bidding on them. My eyes widened in shock. "This muthafucka is selling us?!"

When it was my turn to go, the camera man raised his brows and smiled. "Oh, you gon make Deuce some good money. I know he sampled that pussy." Shaking his head, he said, "C'mon and get in front of the camera girl."

Rolling my eyes, I went in front of the camera while the guys on the screen showed numbers. They shouted and screamed for me to perform different poses for them. "Tell her play with her pussy!" one of the old white guys shouted.

I rolled my neck as if his ass had lost his mind "I'm not doing that bullshit, so you might as well kill me right here!"

The other women gasped at my outbursts. "Girl, just do it," one of them whispered.

"Fuck no!" I spat, just as the door on the opposite side opened up and an angry Deuce walked in, slapping the dog shit out of me.

Falling flat to the floor, he lifted his foot to kick me, but Rochelle screamed out, "She's pregnant Deuce!" Letting his foot drop to the ground, he yoked me up and pulled me into a dark room, tossing me on the floor.

"I told you to stop fucking disrespecting me, Kori. You playing with me and I'ma beat that damn baby outta ya pretty ass. Now, just for showing ya ass, bend over." He looked on with disgust. "So, you don't hear me talking to you?" Still showing no signs of interest, he pulled my hair. Bending me over, he rammed his thick 10-inch dick in me. I yelped out in pain. "Nah, you wanna disrespect me, right?!" Feeling myself get dizzy and lightheaded, everything seemed to get dark and I fell over.

Chapter 44

Andrews

After noticing the woman whom Deuce was handling rough, I instantly recognized her. That was Edo's girl who he brought around once when we had to discuss some business. *This dude has lost his mind, he's already screwed Edo over and now he is doing the extreme*, I thought. I wasn't going to get involved because it could cost me my job but, after hearing Rochelle shout that she was expecting, I knew this wasn't the place she needed to be.

Leaving out the house, I contacted Diesel.

"Yo Andrews, it's good to hear from you." Sarcasm dripped from his voice.

"Listen, I got a lot of explaining to do, but I need you to meet me somewhere like right now."

"I would love to do that, but I got a crisis at hand to handle."

"Diesel, I know it's regarding Kori. Rochelle already let me know that she reached out to you. You can't come here right now; it's too hot. Let me come to you before you jeopardize her life," I warned him.

He sighed into the phone. "Aight man, you better not be fucking with me."

"No, I'm not Diesel. I got you and I know you can't trust me, but I am not going to let him get away with this shit."

Ending the call, I knew how Deuce operated his house of ladies, as he called this shit he had going on. Deuce would bring women who were vulnerable here, promise them a place to stay and shit, fed them, clothed them under the condition that men can buy them for the night. The men had the option of enjoying the women there in their rooms or leaving out to enjoy them. The only way the woman could leave the house and never return was to pay Deuce a large amount of cash up front. As a lawyer partaking in his prostitution ring, I couldn't give him up without incriminating myself but, as much money as Edo paid me, I was definitely going to get his girl out.

Meeting up with Diesel, I gave him the ins and outs of the house. We wouldn't be able to get Kori today because Fridays and Saturdays were his most lucrative days. Sundays, he went home to Marie early in the morning, which was perfect. I knew he wouldn't risk Marie finding out about this spot, so he wouldn't take Kori out the house. His right hand man who was in charge of the camera, Rick, usually napped around 3 or 4pm after he had his coke intake. I wanted to make no mistake in saving Kori from this monster.

"We gon handle this the right way. I'ma get Marie's friend to look out for us too. He's a criminal lawyer and he's building a case against Deuce anyway."

"So, what are they saying about Edo?" He shook his head.

"If we could bring Deuce in, then Edo can get off the hook, but we gotta find a way for him to confess to all that shit he doing cuz you know Edo not into no snitching." Listening to Diesel make sense of the situation, I was devising a plan to take Deuce out.

"Okay, so reach out to the lawyer and call me as soon as he says he's on board to handle this on Sunday." Shaking his hand, I had to head to my office to do some digging of my own to cover my ass, in case Deuce wanted to play stupid.

Chapter 45

Ari

Being arrested had to be the worst thing possible. Everything that I used to do to criminals was being done to me. I thought the cops would show me some mercy being as though I was a fellow female in uniform, but that wasn't the case here. When I was put into the patrol car, the female officer punched me a few times. "You like beating up on women who can't defend themselves, huh?!" We drove around for the longest and, then, I was denied a phone call for 2 days. I was going to really beat Kori's ass for getting me mixed up in this bullshit.

After being in the precinct unable to make a call, the guard finally announced I could do so. I called my captain, hoping he could come get me out but, then, he hit me with some news I wasn't expecting. He informed me that Raj was murdered in his house, shot three times in the chest. Knowing damn well Raj wasn't the type to get mixed up in anything illegal, I figured it had to be Deuce's doing.

When I was finally released, I headed to the apartment I shared with Kori, grabbed up my items and headed straight to New York. Upon arrival, Captain Marcus was waiting for me at his spot. "Aye Ari, this shit gotta stop now. You said you was going to get clean and now I find out you're arrested for putting your hands on a pregnant woman! Have you lost your mind?!"

"No Marcus, listen-"

He cut me off, waving his hands. "No, you listen to me, Arianna. I can't keep doing this shit with you. You act like you wasn't raised correctly,and thank God Kori didn't press any charges against ya stupid ass. Clearly, she's pregnant so that means she doesn't want your ass, so leave her the fuck alone!" he shouted.

Taking everything in that he was saying, I said, "I understand, but I love her and she has to still love me if she went to Pennsylvania with me, so what the fuck? I made a mistake!"

Stomping around the living room, he answered, "No, she doesn't want you. She reached out to me and told me she was only there to help your ass because you had no one." Looking directly in my eyes, he said, "You have to understand, she's in love with the guy she's having a baby by."

"He's locked up on drug charges. What the fuck can he do for her by being in there!"

Marcus shook his head. "Just go put your things down in the room Ari. You're making me exhausted by being this naive or, better yet, stupid." Captain walked out the living room, leaving me to my thoughts.

"I gotta figure this out but, until then, I'ma get me a good night's sleep," I mumbled, heading to the bedroom. I was going to get in touch with Kori and, if we had to raise that nigga's baby together, that's just what was going to have to happen.

Chapter 46

Paris

Bitches just won't learn:

This nigga Deuce had me fucked up if he thought I was going to allow him to talk me into getting rid of this baby. He knew he was fucking me raw; he didn't care about his little prissy ass wife then, so why give a fuck about her now? I had just the right plan to make her leave his ass alone for good. Getting my sonogram print outs and placing them in a box, I was going to pay Marie a special visit that she wouldn't ever forget. Hopping into my car, I called Deuce before I executed my plan. Not to my surprise, he sent me to his voicemail system.

"Oh well," I said while shrugging my shoulders. "I bet he won't take my threats lightly next time." Pulling up my GPS system on my phone, I headed right to Deuce's house. See, one day, Deuce felt the need to violate me and, instead of coming inside to chill like he promised, he headed home, not realizing I was following him. That was his first mistake, cuz he swore I was this ditzy chick who was fucking with Edo, but I was smarter than I led on.

Pulling up a block away from his spacious mini mansion, I seethed while walking up to the driveway. Carrying the small box that contained sonograms and pictures of me and Deuce in many occasions, I placed it on the doorstep. Turning to walk away, I got to the end of the driveway and thought of all the shit I had put up with Deuce for the last year. "This selfish bastard has hurt me for the last time," I mumbled before pulling the rock I had in my purse out and throwing it at the door with all the anger I'd mustered up.

Running to the side, I waited until I saw Marie come out looking around. A smile crept across my face just thinking of how the news would break her heart. "Look at her, thinking she's the perfect wife with the perfect life," I mumbled, watching her open the box. Pulling out the pictures, the look of hurt showed on her face. She must have glanced at the pictures of us in any and every position there was because she dropped the box, and the tears began to pour out of her eyes. Thinking welp, that was easier than I thought, she opened the door and kicked the box in the house.

Once the coast was clear, I jogged back to my car and headed back to the hotel I was staying at. Knowing Deuce would come look for me or my family, I sent my mother away outta state in the house I had recently purchased on his and Edo's dime. I'd be damned if he sent his boys after us once this got back to him, but I had to teach him a lesson.

Marie must of called him because the minute I heard my phone ring, I saw it was Deuce calling. Not seeing the first call, it rang again. "Gotcha right where I want you!" I said to no one in particular.

Chucking, "Yea, now you can call me and talk huh, just the other day it was fuck me right Deuce!" I chanted, getting myself worked up. After the third call, I answered "Yo!"

"Bitch, have you lost your fucking mind!"

"Deuce, get off my line with the disrespect," I taunted him in the worst way.

"You're a dead woman, I hope you know. Don't let me catch your ass, Paris!"

"Are you done?!" I asked, ready to laugh in his face.

"Am I done? Paris, you have tried to play with me for the last time. You brought that shit to my wife; I promise you, your days are numbered!"

"Aight Deuce, I gotta go, so go wipe your wife's tears nigga!" Hanging up before he could respond, I knew I had got under his skin. I had about 3 hours to get ghost before he caught up with me or sent someone after me.

Chapter 47

Edo

After speaking to Diesel, I found out Kori was indeed alive; she just wasn't safe. The shit crushed me knowing that I couldn't do a thing to help her without risking her life in the process. Andrews came to visit me and gave me the run down on everything that was going on. Deuce was playing with me by involving Kori in his vendetta against me. Watching Kaine walk through the door, I watched his expressionless face and wondered what the hell was he about to say.

"Wassup Edo?"

"Ain't shit, you got something for me?"

"Yea, your boy Andrews reached out to me with a plan to get this shit handled, so we could get your girl unharmed."

Rubbing my tongue across my teeth, I started having ill feelings about this. "So, where does he have her?"

"Apparently, Andrews said he got her stashed in some house out in Long Island that he uses as a prostitution ring and sell the women for money," Kaine said through gritted teeth.

I sat there, unsure of what to think of my uncle. "So, you mean to tell me he think he some type of pimp and he selling my girl's pussy to fuck niggas." I pounded my fist on the table.

"Listen Edo, try to calm down. Andrews said he hasn't let any other nigga have her yet."

"So, why the fuck he got her there then?!"

Kaine looked off. "I honestly think he wants her for himself."

Pondering what Kaine said, my nostrils flared in anger. *This sick bastard been fucking my girl? The minute I get outta here, he's a dead man, on everything,* I thought.

"Have you spoke to your aunt?" he asked, catching me off guard.

"Not today, why?!"

"She told me Deuce got a baby on the way with some girl named Paris; she said you should know her."

Looking at him through squinted eyes, I asked, "Why she think that?"

"It's not thinking. The chick left a box of pictures of her and Deuce fucking and sucking." I shook my head in disgust. "And there were sonogram pics and messages from her telling Deuce she was pregnant by him."

Beyond annoyed with all the shit going on in this circle, I asked, "So, when are y'all going to get Kori? I don't understand why y'all don't just go in there guns blazing, shit!" Kaine looked at me like I was crazy.

"Listen, I'm sure they ain't tell you from the way you're acting, but Kori's pregnant and-"

That's all I heard before I jumped up ready for war. "I need to get out of her yo!"

Shouting, the guards came in. "Is everything aight?"

Kaine faced him. "Yea, he just got some unexpected news."

Nodding his head, the guard left out. "So, she pregnant for real? And tell me that nobody touched her."

Kaine looked at me. "Andrews said Deuce slapped her around a bit."

Hearing that Kori was pregnant with my baby and getting beat on, possibly raped made my blood boil. I had to get this nigga Deuce in here, so I could bounce. Sitting up, I said, "I'm out, keep me posted on everything." I wanted to be the strong man I'd always been, but thinking about Kori has me feeling some type of way. Not the one to cry, I think the last time I shed a tear was when my mama died so, when I got back to my cell and the tears fell, I knew Kori meant the world to me. The fact she was going to be bringing my baby into this world only heightened my love for her.

I just needed to hear her voice and make sure she and the baby were fine. When I met Kori, she was this delicate woman and I could only imagine how the situations she been into would change her. I knew Kori was a fighter, so I knew if there was ever a time she would have to give up, it wouldn't be without a fight. Dropping to my knees, I prayed and hoped that the most high was watching over her. Not one to follow religion this was my last resort and finding some type of strength.

Picking up the phone to call Diesel, I was ready to take care of Deuce and get my baby girl and all the other woman free. Learning that Rochelle worked for Deuce had me leery, but Diesel said although Kori had been beating a few times for her mouth, she wasn't raped or sold like most of the other women. "Yo bruh, Rochelle said she ain't been around the other dudes, but Deuce has been up under her ass since she got there."

"I can't believe Auntie still with this nigga, I wonder if she down on it too."

The news was clouding my judgement and, at this point, no one could be trusted.

"Yo, I hope you don't think auntie foul. She seem to had moved on to this dude Kaine, so I doubt auntie would accept some prostitution bullshit Deuce got going on."

Hearing Diesel out, I said, "Yea, I know, but just the thought that she stuck around this nigga for this long and not know about this. Did you suspect this?"

"Nah, see how that works, Deuce is a fucking weasel and he playing everyone he could. Shit, he got Andrews caught up in the bullshit by covering his ass. He made sure Andrews fucked one of them broads, so he wouldn't go down alone."

"Yea, I heard, but check this out. Keep me posted on my wifey and have Rochelle keep tabs on her."

"No doubt bro, hold ya head."

Ending the call, I had a bad feeling about how this shit was going to play out.

Chapter 48

Rochelle

House calls:

Putting Diesel and Edo up on game to what was going on in the house was putting my life at risk, but I couldn't sit around and see this girl being mistreated. Yes, her sister and me had our run ins, but she wasn't her and she looked like a scared young girl, so I couldn't fault her for Kristen sleeping with my baby daddy.

"Rochelle, come here and clean her up. She needs a shower and I advise you talk some sense into her stubborn ass!" Deuce shouted.

I jumped to my feet and rushed to the room in the basement before he could call my name again. After he took Kori in the room and she started screaming, he made everyone leave. Worried to as what sight I would see when I walked in, I braced myself.

"I'm here." Smelling the air, which reminded me of piss, I noticed Kori balled up in the corner on the floor.

"Don't just stare at her, get her cleaned and in her room." He began to walk out the room. "Take her up the back way. I don't want them other hoes looking at her," he instructed.

I could only imagine what her face looked like because I saw the red marks on her legs and arms. Shaking my head, "Kori, it's just me in here," I whispered, touching her shoulder. She looked up at me with tears running down her face, a bloody nose and lip; one of her eyes were black and blue.

"Why is he doing this to me?!" her voice trembled. Holding in my tears, I helped her up.

"Diesel is coming for you, baby girl. I don't know what's wrong with this sick bastard, but I promise you we are going to get you out of here!" I warned her while lifting her to her feet. "Did he hurt your stomach?"

"No, the baby is my fine. He didn't rape me vaginally, only anally, and tried to get me to give him head and, well, that's why I got beat up. I refused," she stressed. "I can take anything, but I'm not sucking his dirty dick. A few months ago, I was a virgin, and now I'm pregnant and being pimped out by my baby's uncle," she chuckled, trying to make light of the situation.

"Girl, I'm glad you can smile through all the bullshit." I looked at the hurt in her eyes.

"I'm never leaving here. I've already prepared myself mentally to go through this shit for as long as I'm pregnant. I just hope he has the decency to at least get me good care during my pregnancy."

Grabbing her face to look at me, "Don't say that shit Kori. Edo is going to make sure you're outta here," I reassured her. She smiled weakly at me while I helped her to her bedroom. Entering the room, I laid a pants pajama set down.

"I can shower, you don't have to help me," she said, but I honestly didn't want her outta my eyesight.

"I'll just sit on the toilet then, but I'm not leaving you alone." Kori took longer than I expected showering, but I could hear her crying lightly.

I got up to go sit on the bed, when I felt a faint vibration under the mattress. Pulling out her Apple Watch, I answered the call. "Hello." Listening to the automated system, I waited until Edo voice sounded on the other end. "Edo, hold on, it's Rochelle." Rushing into the bathroom, "Kori, it's Edo," I whispered.

She grabbed the watch so fast out of my hand. "Hey papi," she cried. I told her I was going to watch the door to make sure no one heard her. Relieved that she was able to take that call when she exited the bathroom, she looked a little happier, so I knew that Edo must of told her some good news. "Thank you." She hugged me tightly.

"No doubt, baby girl. I gotta get outta here. I'ma charge your watch though. I'll drop it back off in a few." She nodded her head when there was a knock on the door. "She's ready." Kori looked at me weird. "It's the doctor to check on you." She breathed a little lighter.

Chapter 49

Kori

The Doctor is in...

Watching Rochelle leave out and a doctor walk in, I watched her like a hawk. She was an older African American woman, very pretty and something about her seemed familiar, but I couldn't place where I'd known her from. "Can you lay down for me please?" she instructed as she looked in her rolling suitcase she brought along. Doing as I was told, I eased myself on the bed. Between my ass hurting and my face feeling like it was being stomped on, my stomach wasn't harmed. "How many months are you?"

"Almost four months." She nodded. "So, are you taking care of my face or just checking the baby?" I was curious.

"I was only instructed to check on the baby, your face should heal on its own."

Sucking my teeth, "This muthafucka," I mumbled.

She looked up from her bag. "Is something wrong?"

I leaned up on my elbows. "Yes, there's a lot of things wrong here. I'm fucking pregnant, being raped and beaten every chance this muthafucka feel like it and, yet, he wanna check on my baby that belongs to his nephew!" I was getting myself worked up.

"Shh, calm down," she tried to hush me, but I was tired of being quiet.

"Are you a licensed doctor? How could you come here to check me out, knowing what the hell is going on in this place?" I spat.

"Listen, Kori, that's your name, right?" she asked.

"Yea."

"I get paid to make sure everyone here is healthy. I don't know what's going on in here because that's not my duty, I'm in and out."

Glaring at her, I said, "So, now that you know, are you going to get me out of here?"

"Sweetie, as much as I would love to get involved, I just can't do that. I'm sorry."

Looking at her as if she lost her mind, I said, "Bitch!" I rolled my eyes before falling back on the bed, letting her check on the baby.

Tuning her exam out, she asked, "Do you want to know what you're having?"

"Why? What difference would it make?"

"Okay, I'll take that as a no." Ignoring her existence, she continued, "Okay, your cervix and everything is intact; the babies' heart rates are normal."

"Babies? As in multiple?"

She looked up at me from the monitor and started pressing down on my stomach, causing some discomfort. "I asked you did you want to know, but you seemed to give me an attitude so…"

Sighing heavily, "I apologize, this is just stressing me out. I'm scared" I began to cry.

"It's going to be okay." The nurse came around trying to soothe me, but nothing at this moment would make me feel better. "You're having twins Kori; you have to be strong for them babies." I tried to stop the tears from falling. "I'll be checking you out until you give birth Kori so, even if you think you're alone, I'll be here," she assured me. "Do you want a print out of them?"

"Yes please." After she finished preforming the exam, she allowed me to hear their heartbeats and started packing up her items. "Can you at least tell him to feed me please? I'm starving."

"He hasn't been feeding you?"

Shaking my head no, I answered, "He says my mouth is reckless, so I have to suffer."

Watching her demeanor change, she said, "I'll get him to feed you, that I can control. You take care and here's my card. If you feel a slight discomfort, you have them give me a call." I nodded. "Kori, I don't care what time it is, you hear me?" Looking at her smiling as she left, she said, "And don't call me nurse. Call me Danielle." Reaching in her purse, she handed me some potato chips. My stomach growled as I thought about the sour cream and onion flavor.

Once she was out of the room, I devoured the chips in less than 5 minutes. Waiting on someone to interrupt me, I thought about Edo and the hopes he promised me. "Bae, I'm trying to get you out of there as soon as I can, so try to hold tight for daddy. I know that nigga treating you like shit but, trust, Rochelle has your back so, if you need anything, let her know and I'm going to see to it that it gets done."

For just the moment, talking to him made me forget about all that I was going through. Rochelle let me know she would be returning before her shift was over with my watch, so I could hear Edo talk to me since I had to keep my voice down. I couldn't wait to let him know we were expecting twins. As much as I wanted to fight Deuce and try to escape, I knew that my babies didn't deserve to be put through more stress than what they were already dealing with. Danielle informed me that she would be visiting me once a week to check on the progress. Something about her seemed so familiar, but I just couldn't understand where I had knew her from. I probably saw her around before because she sure didn't act like she knew who I was, so I tried to dismiss the idea. "It will come back to me, I'm sure."

Hearing knocking on the door, it was Rochelle; she came with food on a tray and flicked her arm in my direction, displaying my watch. Smiling at her, I mouthed "Thank you." After she left, I thought, *I don't understand why her and Kristen couldn't get along but, then again, maybe the dick was just that damn good that Rochelle couldn't let it go.* I chuckled before knocking out with my watch on, waiting for his call.

Feeling the vibration on my arm, I jumped up, only to notice that the door was slightly ajar. Picking up the call, my heart beat rapidly while trying to see if someone was outside the door listening. "Bae, bae," I heard Edo speaking. I tried my best to whisper as I put my Bluetooth in my ear.

"Babe, my door is open. I can't talk but I'm here." Hearing his voice soothed me a little.

"I can't believe this shit yo. Listen ma, I swear I'm not going to allow you to stay there too much longer, even if I have to get you out of there myself!"

Noticing the light by my bedroom door flick on, I pulled the blanket over me. "I'm having twins," I whispered. "Somebody is coming so just listen, okay?"

I watched as Deuce came in the room. "I'm leaving out for a few days, don't try nothing stupid Kori. I would hate for you to lose that baby." A smile crept across his face and I just nodded, hoping he would leave me alone. "When I come back, I'ma need to swim in that tight ass pussy of yours too." Almost throwing up in my mouth, I grilled him.

"Oh, hell no, this nigga getting real loose with his lips," I heard Edo say as Deuce left out, shutting the door closed.

"He's gone Edo."

"Yo Kori, I'm so sorry you going through this shit, but I may have to do something you're not going to be happy with." Perking up, I knew Edo was only trying to get me outta there. "I need you to answer the phone for Ari and act like you're sorry. I'm telling you this because we going to need the cops on your side for when you get out of there," he instructed.

Not really wanting to communicate with Ari at all, I knew Edo was right. "Okay babe, I trust you."

"Good, now get you some sleep. I'ma give Rochelle the instructions so that we can get this plan together. Oh and Andrews is coming to see you real soon."

"Okay." The machine alerted his time was almost up.

"Kori, I love you and, the minute I get out, I'm marrying your thick ass."

Chuckling, I said, "I love you more Edo, but that better not be no damn proposal cuz I'm not accepting that weak ass shit." We both laughed before we were disconnected. Feeling the flutter in my stomach, I drifted off to sleep, happy that Deuce wouldn't be around for a few days.

Chapter 50

Marie

Deuce had a way of really getting me pissed off and, after that nasty hoe left a box in the front of my house with pictures of the both of them, I was beyond over his shit. Kaine told me I was more than welcome to come stay at his house and, at that moment, I put his invitation to use. Deuce had been calling my phone nonstop trying to plead his case, but I didn't have no fight left in me. Having my lawyers draw up the divorce papers, he was going to be mad when he found out that I was coming for the company that we built together as young adults. He could go be with Paris' ass and raise that baby with her because I wanted nothing to do with that situation.

Edo had not been reaching out to me and, according to Diesel and Andrews, he sure kept in touch with them. Little did he know, I was paying his ass a visit. As much as I was doing to get his little narrow ass out, he better not disrespect me ever again. Hell, I raised him and didn't even raise my own children. Walking into the jail, I waited for him to be escorted in. When he came in, the blood looked like it drained from his face.

"Surprised Eladio?" I asked sarcastically.

"Yea, I wasn't expecting a visitor, let alone you," he spat.

Not one to hold my tongue, I said, "What the hell is your problem and why haven't I heard from you?" He sat across from me just staring, as if I was boring him. "Did you not hear me, boy?"

Sitting up to the table, he responded, "I'm trying to see when you was going to tell me that you was creeping on Deuce?"

I was taken back by his straight forwardness. "I don't owe your ass an explanation. Have you forgotten I'm the damn adult here and you will respect me!" I said through gritted teeth.

"See, that's where you're wrong auntie. I'm not a damn kid and, instead of you coming to me and telling me, you just found the next nigga to fuck with?"

"Let me tell your black ass something Eladio. Your uncle has been treating me like shit for years. I been planned on divorcing him but, when I started putting pieces together about his dealings and shit, I knew I had to cover my back so, in the process of filing for divorce, I met Kaine, whom I've actually started fucking with after your uncle raised his hand to me." I watched his facial expression and stopped him before he could respond.

"So, the next time you want to question me, come correct cuz I'm not none of these inexperienced females you be messing with!"

Getting up, I was over the visit and Edo could kiss my ass and help goodbye. "Auntie wait, I never knew," he said with sincerity in his voice.

"Nobody knows. I've kept that shit a secret because I never wanted my husband to look bad to anyone or even hear I told you so's from people I know, but that doesn't excuse the way you've been treating me as if I'm the enemy."

"You're right auntie. I just been hearing some shady shit about Deuce and, knowing that you're married to him, I wasn't sure how you aren't aware of these things going on?"

"Things going on, what are you talking about?" I asked, not understanding what Edo was saying.

"When Deuce leaves for the weekends, where does he go auntie?"

"To the company's office Edo. C'mon, you know that," I chuckled but he seemed unamused.

"Nah, he doesn't, but do me a favor. When you leave here, check this number; it's registered to a house in Queens. I can't give you the address yet, but my girl is there."

"Edo, what girl? You been talking about her for a few weeks now and, if she's your girl, then why haven't she been up here or, better yet, why haven't I met her, but I met that hoe Paris, who by the way is having your uncle's child," I spat.

Edo looked like he was worried and then he explained to me that his girl couldn't come see him but that she was somewhere and, in due time, I would meet her. With Edo leaving me out of the loop, I wanted to curse him out, but I knew Edo and I was pretty sure right now he felt like he couldn't trust me.

"What's your girl name? Can I at least know that?"

"Yea, her name is Kori." It was at that moment that I needed to do some research of my own.

"Aight auntie, don't forget to call that number and then I'll give you the run down." Leaving out of the visit, I was anxious to get in touch with Kaine.

Heading straight to his office, I saw that his new receptionist was there. I hoped she didn't try to stop me from entering his office. Spotting Kaine in the hallway, "Kaine, have you found out anything on Kori?!" I shouted in his direction, cussing him to turn around.

"Huh?!" he asked. His receptionist jumped up from her seat.

"Kaine, can I talk to Marie really fast?"

Annoyed that this girl was interrupting what I wanted to talk to him about, "Yea, Marie, I'll be in my office," Kaine said, turning to walk away.

"Not to be rude sweetie but-,"

"Jada, my name is Jada," she said and, before I could speak, she said, "You're Kori's mother, right?"

The way she looked at me, I was intrigues. "How do you know Kori?" I asked.

"I'm Kristen's best friend."

"How do you know I'm her mother?" She pulled out her phone, displaying pics of my daughters who were so beautiful.

"Kori favors you so much and, well, Kristen definitely has your attitude." She smiled and then it disappeared when she came across another pic.

"Which one of them is pregnant?"

"Kori." That's when her eyes began to water. "She's pregnant and well..."

"Jada, what the hell was so damn urgent?" a female voice came from behind, causing me to whip around and, when I laid eyes on her, I passed out.

Chapter 51

Kristen

A moment of truth

Looking down at the floor, "Kaine, come get ya damn woman!" I shouted. "Jada, what happened to her?" Jada was fanning Marie, who was lying on the floor.

"She passed out when she saw her daughter."

Shrugging, I chuckled.

"Her daughter?!" Kaine raised his brow in Kristen's direction.

"Hi." She waved at him.

"Damn, I didn't know she had any children."

Shrugging, I said, "That's a long story." Kaine lifted Marie up as she came back to her senses.

"Wait Kaine, let me talk to her for a minute," she said, pointing at me.

"No babe, come sit your ass down for a few. Kristen, please don't go anywhere," he begged her.

"Oh, trust me, I'm not," I assured him.

"Jada, what the fuck? How did you know she was my mother?"

Jada instructed me to follow me. "Okay, the first day she came in here, I knew something about her was familiar, but I couldn't figure out what it was. Then, when Kaine introduced me to her as Marie Samuels, I did some snooping of my own on his computer," Jada told me, showing me the screens. "He told me she was his high profile client, which I knew to be not true because I've met them all, but I saw them flirting and I heard their fuck session in his office." Jada laughed, thinking about that day.

I looked at Jada with the you know you crazy look. "Bitch, you heard them?!"

I laughed. "Yea but, anyway, so after looking for a Marie, I came up empty handed but, when she left, it dawned on me that she favored Kori a little, so I just decided let me type in her name Kori and then I used her current last name." Jada showed me her computer. "Bam, there she is; she's hiding from somebody and I just so happen to figure out who it was."

I shook my head. "Why are you a receptionist and not a cop, bitch?" She laughed.

"Cuz I can't stand them pigs."

"So, who is she hiding from? And why?" Jada shrugged.

"Why don't you ask her that yourself because here she comes," I said, pointing in the direction of Kaine's office. What now?

Marie came flying down the hallway. "Marie, try to be easy!" Kaine yelled after her, but she was not trying to hear that.

"Kristen! Come here."

I looked over at her and then back at Jada before walking in her direction. "Can we talk somewhere private?" I asked, walking off.

"Y'all can go in my office," Kaine said.

Following her to his office, the minute the door closed, I broke my silence. "How could you leave us?! You been living the fucking life, and now my sister is missing and pregnant. Grandma died, like what the fuck mommy?" I shouted, letting my emotions get the best of me.

"Kristen, mija, please let me explain to you-"

I raised my hand. "Explain? Explain what? How you were a dead beat mom and how papi is locked away until who the fuck knows when!" I wasn't giving her a chance to try and make me believe any of the bullshit coming from her mouth.

"Kristen, okay, listen. I deserve all of this lashing, but you're not going to keep being disrespectful towards me. Let me explain to you why I gave your grandmother custody of you and Kori before you go passing judgement on me."

Just as I sat down to hear her out, Diesel and Kaine came flying in the office. "We have to go Kristen."

"Diesel, how do you know my daughter?"

Looking from Diesel to my mother, he asked, "Auntie, how do you know Kristen?"

At that moment, I was so lost with everything that was going on. "Don't tell me I been fucking my cousin this whole time, cuz I'm in love with this fucker!" I said, pointing to Diesel.

"No, I'm married to Deuce." The room became so silent, you could hear a pin drop.

"This is some sick shit, so you're married to the man who has been pimping out my pregnant baby sister?!"

My mother looked at me as if I was crazy. "Come again Kristen?!"

"Deuce has Kori and she's pregnant by his nephew Edo. Oh and yea, your husband, the nigga you been shacking up with, has my sister someplace fucking her and pimping her," I spat, getting in my mother's face. I didn't want to be disrespectful but, knowing she was married to him, I had to blame somebody and, right now, she fit the criteria. Turning to leave out, I had enough of the bullshit they had going on. "Jada, let's go, I need to find my sister!" I waved in her direction.

"Rochelle said she's doing fine. Andrews is getting things in order to get her."

With all that Diesel said, all I heard was his ratchet baby mama's name. "Rochelle? So, this bitch is down with this sex ring too?" Leaving out, I hopped in my car, slamming the door shut. Jada hopped in just in time before I left her back there with the circus.

"So, you don't want to hear them out?" she asked.

"Unless they're talking about getting Kori right now, no!"

Jada dropped the conversation.

Chapter 52

Deuce

After I couldn't locate Marie, I started growing impatient. *Where the hell is she?* I thought as I searched our house and then our vacation house in Connecticut. Thinking all this shit started because of Paris, I went to her house and saw an eviction notice on the door. "So, this bitch started drama, then trying to ghost me." Pulling out my phone, I called Donald, my private investigator. Hopefully, he had something on this girl's whereabouts.

"Deuce, how can I help you?"

"Yo Donald, I need to locate my baby mother; she trying to ghost me and not let me be in my child's life," I said, trying to sound convincing.

"Give me her name and as much information as you can on her, so I can get to work." Rambling off Paris' information to him, he told me he would give me a call in a few hours. Waiting on his call, I would go searching for my wife who was mad because of Paris.

When I pulled up to the studio, I noticed Diesel's car parked out front, but he was heading back out. "Yo Diesel, you seen your aunt?"

"Nah Unc, last I saw her was a few days ago."

Nodding my head, I let him pass by. "You thought about what I said?"

"Oh yea, I did, so when you want me to do this meeting?"

"In a week, I'ma give you all the information. Let me tie up some loose ends on this side."

"Copy."

Watching him leave, something about Diesel was off, but I couldn't place my finger on what it was; maybe it was because I was doing some crazy shit, but I felt like everyone was out to get me.

Looking at my ringing phone, I answered, "Yo!"

"Deuce, did you tell Andrews he could place a bet on Kori? Cuz his ass talking about he want a night with her and that you approved of this!"

Not believing what I was hearing, "Hell no, I said nobody fuck with her; she is not up for grabs. Are y'all fucking stupid?" I asked, jetting to my car.

"Aight," he ended the call.

"What the hell is wrong with people!" I put my car in drive, heading straight to the house where I left a few of the girls at a time.

Chapter 53

Kori

Hearing all the commotion in the house woke me out of my sleep. Grabbing the clothes that I wore to the house, I knew some shit was about to pop off and I needed to be ready for whatever. "Deuce ain't say shit about you getting her!" I heard a dude yell.

"Nigga, I paid my money, so I'm taking that bitch with me. He think he the only one who gets to sample her, when we are the reason this spot is still making him money!" I heard another dude yell.

"Andrews, you better not step foot in that room!"

Hearing the dude say Andrews' name, I got excited. Sighing, Edo was definitely winning me over by pulling his luck to save me and his babies. I just may take him up on that proposal behind bars.

"If you step foot in her room, I'm going to kill you!"

"Kill me? Do you know I'm a lawyer and this will be the first place they look for me if I go missing," he assured the dude.

"I'm telling you, if you step any closer, you will-" and the next thing I knew, I heard a loud thud hit the floor but no gunshots. Scared to move from the spot, I heard the dude who was talking to Andrews.

"Aye, help me move this fat muthafucka to the basement."

"His ass too heavy. Kick him to the side. I hit his ass with the gun; he gon be out for a minute."

Covering my mouth with my hands, I contemplated jumping from the window, but I knew the babies wouldn't survive that jump. Running to the door, I locked it before the guys could enter.

"Open this door bitch. Deuce on his way, so I suggest you act like you know before he beat ya pretty ass again," one of them laughed.

"I'll open it when he comes back!" I shouted. "So, leave me alone!"

"Shit, I ain't got time to be arguing with her ass, now help me move him."

Listening to them move Andrews from the front of the bedroom, a crashing sound came from downstairs. "What the fuck now?" I hurried and unlocked the door, just in case it was Deuce. I couldn't afford another ass whooping.

"Kori, let's go!" he shouted from the staircase. He must have taken the steps two at a time because he was at my room in no time. Pulling me by the hair before I could protest, he escorted me to a van with black windows.

"Just when I thought I was going to be set free," I mumbled.

"Don't say nothing to me, Kori. I'ma just have to kill you," he instructed. "As much as I love that pussy, I'm not about to risk getting caught up fucking with you!" He jumped in the driver's seat and placed a pistol in the middle console. "Mike, let's go!" he shouted. Watching another dude hop into the passenger seat, I could only imagine where they were taking me.

I didn't even get to see Rochelle before I left or the doctor. I'm never going to get away from this stupid fuck.

Driving at a high speed, I put my seatbelt on. If he wanted to die, I was not about to let him take me with. Looking in the mirror at him, he kept eyeing me. "You ain't gotta be scared. I'ma take real good care of you," he said. I looked over at this Mike character he had with him.

"Yo boss, I don't know why you just don't let her ass go; she ain't no good to you," he laughed. "She having your nephew baby; what chu gon do, raise it as yours?" he asked, laughing.

Deuce must not have found it funny because he pulled the car over and looked and asked Mike to repeat himself. Mike said the same shit again and that's when Deuce pulled out the pistol from the console and let off a shot to his head. "Oh, my God!" I screamed, covering my mouth. I couldn't believe he just killed this dude in front of me.

Deuce looked back at me. "You better shut up and wipe your face." Taking heed to what he said, I wiped the blood splatter from my face and sat in the seat directly behind him. I didn't want to be that close to a dead body. "Kori listen, I ain't trying to kill you, but don't push me right now."

"I understand." Trying to avoid conversation with him, he jumped back on the highway and drove to a wooded area. Hopping out of the car, he pulled Mike out of the passenger seat and kicked his body down the hill. Watching him go to the trunk of the car, he popped it before getting something to clean the inside of the window and seat.

"You wanna come sit up front?"

Shaking my head no, I said, "I'm good back here."

Seeing his phone light up, it alerted a call from wifey. "Baby, where are you?" Only hearing a female talk and not being able to make out the words, his face turned to a scowl. "The fuck you mean you want a divorce?" He went silent again. "Oh, so you think it's just that easy to walk away from me, huh? Nah Marie, you got another thing coming if you think I'm giving your ass a divorce."

Looking in my direction, he said, "Oh, you want me to let you go? I told you that bitch is lying about the baby!" She must have hung up on him. "Fuck!" I turned my head not to make eye contact with him. "Let me get rid of you so I can get back home to my fucking wife."

Furrowing my brows, I didn't know what he meant by get rid of me, especially not after he just committed a murder in my eyes. The panic started to set in and we were back on the road. "Please God, get me away from this lunatic. Shit Edo, why the fuck did I have to meet you? Ari, why the fuck did you have to beat my ass, owe this bastard money and sell me to pay your fucking debt. Mommy, had you not left my grandmother to raise me, she would be alive and I would probably be with a good wholesome dude and working with a family," I mumbled, looking at all the street signs I passed until I ended up falling asleep.

Chapter 54

Marie

Calling Deuce was not something I wanted to do but, knowing that I could track his location if I stayed on the phone with the bastard for more than a minute, I did it to save my daughter. Finding out that Kristen and Kori was right under my nose the whole time had me ready to risk it all. I lost them once and I'd be damned if I lose them again. Romero, their father, was locked up and, before his angry ass got out, I wanted to get close to my babies so they could ride out with me.

Learning Kori was kidnapped by Deuce was not what I was expecting when I asked Kaine to locate them. She was pregnant by my nephew and probably somewhere being tortured. We had Andrews and Rochelle as the inside people but, when we got to the house, we found him knocked out in the basement with a knot on his head, and Rochelle wasn't there when it all went down. I searched every room until I realized she wasn't there anymore. Kristen wanted nothing to do with me and, although I was salty, I knew had it had been the other way around, I'd probably act the same damn way.

"I found something," Jada said from an upstairs bedroom. Rushing up there, it was a Bluetooth headset and a picture of the sonogram. Holding it up, I saw the two sacks and realized I was going to be a grandmother of two babies. As much as I wanted to hold in the tears, I cried because I didn't know what Deuce was doing with her.

"Why you crying? You act like you raised us!" Kristen spat, looking in my direction.

"Kristen, I know you're mad."

"Nah, I'm not mad, I'm pissed the fuck off. You here crying while you don't even know a damn thing about Kori but her fucking name!"

"Kristen c'mon, you're being a lil too harsh on her. You haven't even heard her side of the story," Kaine said in my defense.

"I don't care about her side," Kristen said, leaving out. "Are you going to track this nigga or you fucking with us, Marie?"

"Kristen, yes, I'm going to track him," I said with a sigh. "Let's go." Leaving out, I grabbed the picture and headed to my car. Diesel caught up to my stride.

"Auntie, she's hurting. She has been spazzing on everyone, even her best friend' her and Kori is like two peas in a pod."

"I know Diesel. I'm not mad; I just wish she would give me a damn chance to explain." Pulling out his phone, Kaine called some cop named Ari to start locating where Deuce was headed.

Chapter 55

Kori

You gotta be quicker than that

Waking up just as Deuce was stopping for gas, "Yo, you hungry?" he asked.

"Yea." I shrugged, trying to focus on where we were. Looking for any street signs, I just spotted a gas station and a spot called The Cookout. "Where the hell are we?" Deuce was fidgeting with his phone before shutting it off all together. Falling back into the seat, I just wanted somebody to come and get me from this creepy nigga. Deuce placed an order of burgers, then headed back to me.

"Eat this and then I'ma let you go pee."

"Okay."

Deuce put the car on cruise control while the radio played. "This track is coming from Washington's hottest newest rapper." My ears perked up. Lying down low in the seat, I checked my watch, keeping the brightness on low. Kristen had texted me, asking if I was okay. The next message shocked me.

Kristen: guess who I came in contact with? Our mother Marie

Rereading the message a few times, I couldn't believe what she had said. Trying to type quickly, I replied: wow

That's when the light on my watch brightened to its highest settings, causing Deuce to look in my direction. I hid the watch under me. "What the fuck are you doing back there?"

"Nothing, I'm uncomfortable, that's all." I tried to play it off.

"I saw a light," he said, looking in the mirror. Shrugging, I answered, "Maybe it was from outside." Once his eyes were focused back on the road, I hid my watch under my hoodie and sent the location. The light from my watch signaled another text coming through, just as Deuce was looking in the mirror at me.

"You better not move Kori." Stopping the car, he hopped out and pulled me from the seat, but the seatbelt stopped him. "Take that shit off." Doing as I was told, I took off the seatbelt and he pulled me down from the car; that's when the watch fell.

"Son of a bitch."

He picked it up, noticing the incoming text. "So, your ass been sending messages to people this whole damn time." Yoking me up, he pinned me to the car. "Didn't I say don't fuck with me, Kori!" He pulled back his fist and sent a punch to my jaw. Screaming out in pain, I lifted my foot and kicked him as hard as I could in his dick. Sending him bending over in pain, I took my chance to run.

Not knowing where I was going and if I was going to last very long, I was hit with something and everything around me started to fade as I tried to fixate on the bright lights. "Was I dead? Was this the light?" It couldn't be cuz I still heard my heart beating. I heard loud talking, but I couldn't move. Feeling the liquid on my body, I knew it was blood. *I think I lost my babies. I think I'm dying. Why was I going through this?* Was it because he calls me wifey? "I think she's breathing!"

To be continued...

Theresa Reese is a up and coming African American Urban Fiction/ romance author that's sure to make her name known throughout the industry. If you're a fan of thug love stories, hood romance, drama or just a plain ole love story. You'll really enjoy her sassy and classy writing. Cole Hart Signature.

Stay Connected:

Instagram: @mommy_n_me_authors_

Facebook group: Winewitreese

Email: reese326@yahoo.com

Made in the
USA
Middletown, DE